A Mortician's Shadow

Kristal Shanahan

ISBN: 979-8-9913380-8-0

Book Cover by Christy Aldridge

Edited by Meriah Gutterson

Internal Formatting by Savannah R. Fischer

Also By

<u>Featured Anthologies</u>

Scorned

Crumpled

Book Nerd's Community Anthology V.1

<u>Short Fiction</u>

Tormented Sorrows

<u>Collection</u>

Four Seasons of Horror

One

Leaning against the broken tombstone, gazing at the church on the hill that lay in ruin, which was once a central character in urban legends, Justin couldn't help but wonder if the legends had any truth to them. The graveyard embodied a world from the past, in decay and overgrown with grass. He traced the name engraved on the split and weathered tombstone, curious about all the details of the life that ended so long ago. Whittier, the name etched on the tombstone, held secrets that he wanted to unearth. Massive roots from the ancient pine tree that neared fifteen feet in length created several uneven divots in the ground near multiple graves. Justin overheard some town gossip at the local coffee shop that Margaret Whittier was accused of witchcraft and hanged for her crimes on the pine tree's low-hanging branch at midnight on Halloween in 1692. Not only was she hanged, but she was set ablaze afterward. According to the cackling women at the coffee shop, legend stated that the smell of charred flesh wafted from the graveyard toward town at midnight on Halloween, as her soul danced with the devil.

Justin's gaze landed on the church on the hill. Ezechiel Hilltop Church had been a fixture there for decades. The years had not been kind to the aging church. Sentimentality was the primary reason it still stood looming over the graveyard. In the small town of Stahl, nature was left to its own demise, and the church's fall was seen as divinely ordained. As dusk approached, the remaining church walls, one nearly split in half by a recent lightning strike, took on a more sinister appearance. The short walk up the hill was inviting. He felt a pull, as if something was beckoning him to go. He sighed deeply, knowing that he might regret that short walk up the hill. Blowing softly, the grass danced in hypnotic harmony all around Justin as he looked at everything and nothing, all at once.

Secrets of the past were held here, and Justin was determined to discover all the layers of truth, no matter the length of time that it would take. Slowly standing up, he firmly placed his hand on the headstone to steady himself. Gazing across the graveyard to the hilltop church ruins, he noticed movement in the shadows. He blinked a few times, thinking it was his imagination, but the shadows remained, as well as the movement within them. He decided to check it out and cautiously made his way to the church.

Most of the church was in ruins. Two walls remained standing but were weakened by the years of decay and worn from the outdoor elements. Providing a barrier from the graveyard, the walls blocked the view, so Justin had to venture to the unknown around the corner, and he was leery about what lay beyond the crumbling walls. A partial and unstable spiral staircase led down into a basement to whatever lurked in the underground darkness and awaited him. He stood looking at the staircase in awe and was completely dumbstruck that it led to a black abyss of the unknown. The rocks and bricks, which once held up a beautiful small church, lay scattered on the ground as Justin maneuvered his way around the staircase. Looking at broken shards of glass, tree branches, and sparse grass for any clues of the church's history, Justin felt something brush up against his right side, and a firm, icy hand gripped his own. His entire body stiffened and was on high alert.

"Who's there?" Justin whispered and shook his hand loose from something that was there, but couldn't be seen.

He frantically looked around and didn't see anyone or anything. It appeared that he was completely alone, but he knew differently. Yet he felt compelled to continue to explore. He was drawn to this location, and he couldn't put his finger on why. Not seeing anything other than rubble, he walked toward the staircase. Taking out his phone, he clicked on the flashlight and tried to see down to the underground church basement. It was too dark, even with the light, to see anything other than the few steps in front of him. He clicked off the phone and put it back in his pocket. He put the weight of one foot on the first step to see if it would hold. The staircase moaned from the pressure, and he quickly removed his foot. Standing there, unsure of what to do next, he looked around and started to formulate a plan for when he would return. One last glance around the church ruins, and then Justin began his trek to his car. Thoughts started to consume him about what he needed to do today. Being new to Stahl, he felt the need to visit both the graveyard and the cemetery. He knew he would spend a significant amount of time at both, but this place he felt drawn to, felt a connection. Unsure of why, he knew at some point the truth would be revealed as to the need of visiting this place again and the secrets he hoped to uncover or bury more deeply.

Justin was still thinking about what he needed to do as he approached his car, and paperwork was at the top of the list for the mortuary he owned. Being a funeral director and owner was a dark profession, but he loved it. Working with the dead had its benefits. They are quiet in voice but speak in other ways. Preparing someone for their final resting place was an awesome and rewarding responsibility, as far as Justin was concerned. He has been extraordinarily busy lately. Death would always be in infinite supply, and job security is a plus, Justin would always say when he defended his career choice.

Justin thought he stood where his car was parked. Looking around, scratching his head in confusion, he saw that it was now parked on the opposite side of the road, facing the wrong direction. Chills crept in and clutched his heart. His mind was swimming, and he couldn't make heads or tails of what was happening. He didn't waste any time getting in and heading to work. He couldn't wait to get away from the graveyard and church but was already making plans to return. For his next trip there, he needed to see what the stairs led to in the church basement. He checked his phone to make sure he hadn't missed anything important and started his car. As he was leaving the graveyard, he noticed a few black SUVs with tinted windows sitting near the entrance. He couldn't see anyone and was curious about what was going on. He drove by them; the first one broke away from the others and followed him.

Staying close to his bumper, the black Escalade nearly kissed his silver Mercedes for several minutes. Finally, the SUV peeled off on an off-ramp toward a different part of town.

Justin felt that it had been an intimidation tactic, he was curious as to why someone would want to try to scare him. Maybe there was a logical explanation, but he knew he stumbled onto something that he probably wasn't supposed to know about. He really felt like he wasn't supposed to be at the Stahl Graveyard. Halloween was on the horizon, so maybe it had something to do with that, and maybe there was some inkling of truth to the legends passed down and passed around. As Justin continued driving to his business, the York Family Mortuary, his mind kept replaying what happened at the graveyard. He knew he hadn't imagined the icy hand, or his car being moved. Knowing he would need to return soon to understand what happened, he felt relief to be back among the living, mostly. Idling at the stoplight close to his business, he looked over at the car next to him. A black Escalade sat idle with black-tinted windows. The driver's side window was open with only a sliver at the top. Justin couldn't get a glimpse of who the driver was. A cloud of cigarette smoke escaped the SUV. As the light turned green, Justin's heart raced as the SUV kept pace with him. Slowing down, the Escalade moved behind Justin again and was too close for comfort. Pulling into his place of business, he fig-ured that the driver already knew more about him than he wanted to admit.

He parked in front of the mortuary. It was after hours, and the two employees had gone home hours ago. He wanted to get a jump start on some paperwork but was uneasy about exiting the car. Taking a deep breath, he grabbed his brief-case, threw his wallet in it, and stepped out of the car. As he shut his door and locked it, his eyes followed the SUV that parked beside him.

Subtle, he thought, and rolled his eyes.

A man dressed in a black suit commanded Justin's attention. "Mr. York, a word, please."

Justin approached with caution. "What can I do for you?"

"I'm sure you're wondering why I followed you." The man said.

Giving the man a hard stare while fidgeting with his car keys, Justin said, "Yeah, of course. It's a bit problematic, whatever your name is."

"My name isn't important. You need to stay away from the graveyard and church. Do you understand?"

Asking genuinely, Justin said, "Not really. Why do I need to stay away from there?"

"Look, I know you're new here, like you've been here about six months and got your business going mostly from a long distance until you could get here. You've been pretty suc-cessful, from what I can tell. You are well liked in this com-munity already, which isn't easy to do. Just trust me on this. Stay away until after Halloween. That's only a week or so away. Can you do that?" He asked Justin.

"I'll stay away for now. I can't promise I won't go back. But, just so you know, something isn't right at that graveyard and church." Justin said quietly.

"I know, Justin, I know." He turned and walked back to his SUV, got in, and quickly drove away.

Walking inside to his business, he was shaking a bit as he unlocked the front door. Breaking from his routine, he locked the door after closing it. He headed straight to his office, turned the light on, threw his briefcase on his loveseat, and sat in his chair behind his desk. He grabbed a cup from one of the drawers and pulled out his Dewar's scotch. He poured himself a shot and gulped it down in seconds, then poured a second shot. He stared at his computer, feeling exhausted and defeated. He was trying to understand everything that had happened tonight and struggled to wrap his mind around it. Taking a sip of his scotch, he turned on his computer. Instead of doing the paperwork he needed to do, he researched the tombstone name, Whittier, at Stahl Graveyard. Searches returned normal family history, descendants still in the area, and then *bingo*, he thought to himself.

A deep dive into the family name, Whittier, proved fruitful. Justin settled in to read an article on the family he was hopeful to learn more about. A family with mostly daughters in the 1600s, they were shunned because they were thought to be a coven family of witches and warlocks. They were treated horribly, based on assumptions. The community would throw rocks at their home and refuse to let them enter and conduct business in town anywhere. Protests with the townspeople occurred by bringing torches and slanderous words to their home. Hours of angry and destructive protests happened over and over in their front yard. While no one else stood up for them, they stood up for themselves by not leaving as they were so frequently encouraged to do. Rumors were cultivated and created by women who loved nothing more than to gossip and ridicule those who were different. Stahl's homegrown folks enjoyed the sadistic treatment that continuously befell the Whittier's, even though most of them were God-fearing Christians. The Whittier's were being shunned at every turn. In no way were they going to change the minds of the townspeople or how they viewed them.

The family finally decided to keep to themselves much of the time. They began to grow their own food and traveled to the next town over if they needed anything beyond the meals on their table. This was how life for the Whittier's evolved. It was their new normal, and quite lonely. Rumors circulated that two of the daughters ran away because they couldn't stand not having friends or husbands. Most of the stories swirling around Stahl revolved around the oldest daughter and how she snuck out at night and had salacious, secret meetings with the eligible bachelors. She showered them with inappropriate affection and blew enchanted witchcraft whispers up their asses, as the elders in town liked to refer to her actions as.

Something was alluded to in the article that the oldest daughter befell tragedy, but Justin's internet trail ran cold. He sat back and grunted in frustration. His eyes landed on the photo of him with his parents. They were gone now, but he loved daydreaming of the good times that they had. He was an only child, so he didn't have any siblings to connect with. His cousins lived in other states and didn't seem interested in having any type of friendship. It made him sad. Growing up, the family holidays they shared were always fun, and he looked forward to them. As he grew older and everyone drifted apart, he could see that maybe his family wasn't as close as he thought as a child. He always felt like the black sheep of the family and ultimately an utter disappointment to his grandma and grandpa. He wished his grandparents could see his success now, but they likely would judge him for being a mortician. The other cousins were showered with praise and money. Being the oldest, his grandparents felt he should be more adult than necessary. His mom's parents died in a tragic accident when his mom was in college, and he never had the chance to get to know them. Their life viewpoints were positive, as opposed to his paternal grandparents, who had skewed outlooks on life, and he had to learn to live with their disappointment and digs.

At least my parents were amazing, Justin thought.

He knew that it was unlikely for him to meet someone and have children of his own. He was open to it, but he didn't want to get his hopes up. It would take a special woman to live this life with him.

Shutting off the computer, Justin decided that he was done for the night, and he would drive home. He took his wallet out of his briefcase, shoved it in his back pocket, and picked up his keys from his desk. He would leave his briefcase and all his work here. Tomorrow was Sunday, and hopefully, he could enjoy a day of peace. He turned the lights off as he approached the front of the building. After opening the door, out of the corner of his eye, he noticed a black SUV sitting in the parking lot. Locking up, he went directly to his car and began his short drive home. The SUV followed.

Evidently, they were serious about him not returning to the graveyard, he thought.

After Justin was safely inside his home, he began to relax. Looking outside his window, he saw the black SUV drive away from his house. Pulling the curtain closed and locking up made him feel safer, but he felt an unease that he couldn't shake. Since it had been an unusually creepy day, he decided sleep would ease his troubled mind. He made his way toward the stairs after shutting the lights off. Walking upstairs in near darkness, he noticed shadows elongated on the walls and shifting while the stairs creaked and groaned their age. Justin glanced around nervously. His phone began to buzz in his back pocket. He stopped midway on the stairs to answer it. He clicked the green button on his iPhone.

"Hello?" Justin answered curiously.

He wasn't expecting a call. On the other end, loud garbled voices could be heard. Then a whisper.

Ear-splitting static bellowed from his phone while his name was barely audible. "Justin... Justin... Justin."

He quickly clicked it off and shoved it in his back pocket. Thumping hard and thumping quickly, his heart was working overtime as Justin was trying to gain his composure and wrap his head around what had just happened. He finished ascending the stairs to his bedroom, and the lights flickered. No lights were on, as he had turned everything off before he came upstairs. A loud humming noise kept the beat with the light flickering in tandem, and all Justin could do was watch in horror. For the first time in his life, he was uncomfortable being alone. His thoughts flitted back and forth from the icy hand that grasped his at the church to the SUV and the conversation with the mysterious driver, to the shadows he knew he saw at the church, lurking in secret. He felt a deep desire to figure out what was going on, despite the warnings he had received and was receiving now. He moved on to his bedroom and then his bathroom. The lights continued to flicker, but the hum had subsided to a dull, barely audible sound. Grabbing his sleeping pills from the bathroom cabinet, he choked down a couple and drank a few swigs of water from the glass he kept by the sink. He hoped sleep would consume him before his thoughts of the day would. Getting dressed for bed was a quick process, and by the time he crawled into bed, the flickering lights had stopped. He couldn't imagine the light show it put on for anyone who happened to see from outside. He hoped no one saw because he was not prepared to give answers to those types of questions. Sleep came easily for him, though it was troubled.

Elevated nightmares plagued Justin's dreams and played on repeat. Multiple times, he yelled out in his sleep, "No! No! Please, no!"

Each time he woke up in a cold sweat and frantically looked around, thinking he was back at the church and descending into the basement, climbing down the unstable and rickety spiral staircase. After the fog cleared from his mind and he realized he was safe in his bed, he would go to sleep again, only to have the same thing happen again. Giving up on sleep, he decided to lie there and just think and wish for sleep. He closed his eyes, and a sultry male voice whispered,

Justin. Justin, come back to us.

Justin opened his eyes in record speed and scrambled to the other side of the king-size bed. A shadowy figure stood still on the side of the bed he had just crawled away from. An audible gasp escaped his quivering lips. He quickly jumped out of bed and switched on the light. No one else was in the room with him. Frantically looking around, he began to question his sanity, and if what he heard and saw even happened. He switched on the TV in his bedroom and cautiously climbed back into bed, but he was on high alert. He kept the volume low while he watched *Jurassic Park*. His thoughts wandered as he mindlessly watched the movie. He turned the lamp on next to his bed, then got up to turn the overhead light out near the bedroom door. He laid down in the middle of the bed with the remote in hand. His thoughts drifted back to his day as his eyelids grew heavy and he finally drifted off to sleep.

Justin found himself sitting in the graveyard next to the Whittier headstone, running his fingers over the grooves of the letters. The wind howled, and whispers were swirling in the air, but didn't stay long enough for Justin to determine what the words actually were. He didn't understand how he got here, or why he was here again. Justin heard sounds behind him. With trepidation and hesitation, he turned to face the tree that was just a stone's throw away from where he heard the noises. Hanging on the low-lying branch was the young Whittier girl accused of being a witch. Her body was swinging and thumping against the tree, creating the disturbingly rhythmic thumping sounds. Fear settled in and clenched his heart, preventing him from catching his breath. He watched as the body slowed, finally still, until her head turned with a slow, sickening succession of multiple cracks. Her skeletal frame was charred, and her eyes were gone, but the empty sockets held fire. She whispered his name and opened her broken, hanging jaw wide and screamed while bursting into flames.

Justin woke up screaming as loud as a wailing child. Fortunately, he lived alone because it was stupid that he woke up from a nightmare screaming, he thought. His mind drifted, thinking about the nightmare and if it had meaning. He knew on the surface there was something going on, and it was all connected, but he didn't want to think about everything at that moment, not really. He dragged himself out of bed and headed to the bathroom. Brushing his teeth while looking at himself in the mirror, he noticed his bloodshot eyes, the dark circles under them, and his overall haggard appearance. He hadn't been getting enough sleep lately, and now it was catching up to him. He bent down and spat his toothpaste in the sink and rinsed it clean. Looking up at the mirror again, he noticed a shadow in his bedroom that was out of place. He quickly turned to his bedroom to follow the shadow, but it dissipated. He decided to get dressed as quickly as he could so he could go downstairs and have strong black coffee.

Grabbing his first cup of coffee was always a moment that Justin enjoyed. He took the coffee to go sit outside to enjoy being in nature. He had always loved just being outside. First, exploring as a child, but working in the yard or relaxing on his back deck in his comfortable cushioned chair as an adult. Closing his eyes, he tried to clear his mind and concentrate on what he should do today. It was Sunday, and usually his day was filled with work and the occasional funeral, so this was almost an anomaly. He meditated briefly, then continued to drink his hot coffee. He needed to work on his mindfulness, but five minutes was an improvement from last week when he tried meditating. Staring out at the wooded area behind his home, he sat there and just enjoyed being outside until he saw something out of the corner of his eye toward the edge of the woods. A burning smell suddenly filled the air. Looking around, he saw nothing on fire, but it was a putrid smell. Almost like rotting flesh was set ablaze and left to turn to ashes.

Justin. Come join us.

The voice echoed from somewhere in his mind. Setting his sights on a form visible from the trees, he shivered, and goose pimples appeared on his flesh. He knew the voice he heard belonged to whatever was still cloaked in the shadows from a distance. What he didn't understand was how that was possible. The stench was strong, and he coughed for a bit. The form in the trees seemed to move forward like it was coming for him.

Candy, his neighbor, walked over to check on him. "Hey, Justin, you okay? I was outside working in my garden, and I heard you start coughing up a lung there."

Taking a drink of his coffee first, he replied, "Oh, thanks for checking on me. I think I just swallowed wrong. So stupid, but I do that sometimes."

Justin glanced at Candy to see if she bought the lie. He held eye contact with her, giving her his undivided attention.

"Well, I understand. My mom does that all the time." Candy laughed.

She started to walk away and turned back toward Justin. "If you need any help gardening, let me know. Your yard looks a little drab." Smiling with a wink, she was back at her place in a flash.

He couldn't help but think about what it would be like to date her. She was single, but older than him, and absolutely beautiful. Her long, dark brown hair fell past her shoulders, and her green eyes sparkled with unexplored mischief. Maybe he would have the guts to ask her out to dinner someday.

Sighing with relief that the putrid smell was gone, and he didn't choke to death, he got up to go get more coffee and watch the news. As he stood up, a wind whipped through, and a shadow arrived with it, then disappeared just as fast as the wind did. Going inside seemed like the best option at the moment. He had never believed in spirits or ghosts before, but he recognized that something was going on that he couldn't explain. Evil seemed to live here, and it was drawn to him. Even the air felt heavy, and dread crept into his soul. Trying not to be scared and overwhelmed by everything, he needed to decompress.

Inside the house, he made a cup of coffee and poured generously from his Baileys. Plopping down on his couch, he grabbed his remote to turn on the TV and stopped at a local news station to watch what was going on around town.

"A body was found at the church ruins last night. The identity has not been released, but it looks like a murder investigation is underway. In other news, a serious car accident happened right outside of town…"

Justin clicked off the TV. His mind was working overtime, thinking about what he just heard on the news. He felt like he really needed to go back there. He was drawn to the place again, he couldn't figure out why. The last time he was there, unexplained and terrifying events occurred.

Two

The late-morning air was refreshing on the drive back to the graveyard and church. Justin had the windows down and the radio on with the volume low because he enjoyed the quiet. Grateful that the black SUV wasn't watching him any-more, he was able to drive freely without having to worry as much about being followed. Watching the road behind him periodically couldn't be helped, out of sheer paranoia. As he drove, his thoughts drifted to Halloween. One week from today, and the festivities will be in full swing. He planned to invite a few people over, but nothing crazy. He didn't like large crowds, but he enjoyed a good party with a few friends. Maybe he would invite Candy over, or maybe not. He couldn't decide. His thoughts drifted again, but this time they traveled back to the nightmare he'd had. He wondered if it meant anything. He thought maybe something from beyond was sending him a message, although he wasn't quite sure what that was yet.

Pulling onto the street near the graveyard, he parked his car and locked it this time, as he hoped no one would get in it and move it like last time. The sky was overcast, so he didn't need his sunglasses. Unlocking the car, Justin put them in the console. A few seconds later, he locked it again and walked toward the graveyard, which proved difficult. He felt as if a force was pushing against him while he tried to move quicker. Reaching the chain-link fence after what felt like an eternity, he climbed over it to move through the graveyard with ease.

Police tape still marked off where the body must have been. Justin thought about the dream he had and wondered if the person who died here dreamt the same thing. No one else seemed to be here, so the investigation must be over. Everything was eerily quiet, and his body felt like it was on high alert. He looked at the ancient pine tree that loomed over much of the small graveyard with its low-hanging branches and pine needles that frequently fluttered to the ground. Noticing something on the tree, he moved closer. Small rivulets of red ran down the tree and pool at the massive roots that spanned several feet. Touching the red that flowed, he sniffed it, and it held a smell of iron or metal. Justin gasped. He realized that the tree was leaking blood, and he couldn't seem to reconcile what he was seeing with what he knew to be true. He wondered if the dead person saw this too.

Justin, join us.

Running toward his car was the only option at this point, but the whispers followed. Fortunately, his car was where he left it, and, unlocking it, he got in and left as quickly as possible. His thoughts were all over the place as he escaped what may have been an untimely death. He felt skeptical about what was on the agenda for him from what evil forces were at play at the graveyard. Justin decided to go to work and bury himself in the paperwork he knew awaited him. He was going to finish it later in the week, but no time like the present, and he didn't feel like being at home.

Owning the only morgue in town had its benefits, but the drawbacks were definitely how busy he stayed. The body that was recovered the night before would land at his doorstep soon. He missed a message from the coroner, so he likely needed to be at work. Since Stahl was a small town, the communication between the morticians and the coroners was vital.

Sitting at his desk at work and wrapping up the paperwork that he was hoping to finish, Justin received a call.

"Hello, York Family Mortuary, Justin speaking."

"Yes, Justin, it's Bob. I've got that new body for you. Our body transport specialists, Mike and Eli, are bringing the young woman soon, tomorrow, late afternoon at the latest. I'll be there as well because I want to discuss with you what I found; I thought it would be of interest to you."

"I'll stick around later tomorrow then. I anticipated hearing from you today."

"See you tomorrow." Bob hung up abruptly.

Justin hung up the phone. He got up to make sure the cooler was on and at the right temperature for the body that was scheduled to be delivered tomorrow. As he walked into the room, the lights flickered slightly. He wondered if that was a subtle warning for whatever dark forces were at play here in Stahl. He knew the warnings for him would eventually run out and something would happen. He was usually a bit paranoid, but the recent events had made that and his anxiety skyrocket. That combined with what's been happening was not a good combination. The door chimed, signaling that someone was there, so he left the lights on in the mortuary cold room and ventured to the waiting room.

Thursday afternoon, Bob was in the waiting room, looking around. He looked a little nervous and was fidgeting and wringing his hands together.

"Hi Bob, you have the body?"

"No, I drove my own car and wanted to arrive before they got here with her."

"Ah, okay, so what would you like to tell me?"

"The condition of the body is...how shall I say, disturbing. The young woman was in her early twenties and burned to a crisp. It's such a small town that it was easy to figure out initially who we thought it probably was. Her car was left at the graveyard, which made the identification easier. Since her purse was on the front seat, that helped too. We received the dental records and matched it rather quickly. I'm so sorry Justin. It's your understudy, Morgan Webber." Bob looked at the floor with regret and sadness.

"No, oh no. Are you absolutely sure? That can't be! What the hell was she doing out there in the first place?"

Justin ran his hands through his hair and began pacing the length of the room.

"That is what the investigators are putting together. Did you say anything about that place to her?"

Justin spoke with an abundance of anguish, and he couldn't keep it together. Tears streamed down his pale cheeks.

"Bob, I did mention it. I shared with her my experience the other day when I called her to work on her schedule for the next couple of weeks and told her how creepy I thought it was. I warned her to stay away from there and clearly; she didn't heed my warning. This is my fault, thinking that a young person could resist the temptation from seeing that for themselves." Justin shook his head in despair.

Justin's bright blue eyes continued to tear up and he knew he needed to visit Morgan's parents today. He hung his head down, sniffled, and popped his head back up, running his hands through his disheveled brown hair. Feeling distraught and thinking of the uncomfortable moments ahead was distressing to say the least.

Full of emotion, Justin asked, "Were there any other signs as to what caused her body to burn?"

"Nothing. No evidence was left at the graveyard. The police suspect it was intentional and whatever was used was taken with them. That's all they would tell me. I think there's more to it, but that is all the detective friend of mine would say."

"I see. Any idea when the guys will be here with Morgan's body?"

"They just texted me, and it should be any minute. Oh, remember, you'll have to talk to the parents about what type of burial they'll want for her."

"Yeah, Morgan and I actually talked about that once when it was a slow day recently. She wants to be cremated. She knew it was cheaper, and she wanted her ashes scattered somewhere. I'll have to find out from her parents if they're willing to do that."

"Well, it sounds like she has an idea of what she wanted, anyway. Looks like they just pulled up with her. You want to open the door for them, and I'll go make sure everything is good?"

"Sure." Justin slowly moved to the front door of his business. He felt like everything was moving in slow motion.

Mike and Eli wheeled Morgan to the cold room. Justin followed. The cold and clinical room was empty, with only one body to care for.

"Thanks guys. I appreciate it. Can you pull the center door open? I'll add her name to the door in the space to write it in. Go ahead and gently put her on the slab. I'll take it from there."

Mike spoke first. "I'm sorry for your loss. Bob said she worked for you."

"Yeah, she did. She was a great young woman, full of life and expectations for the future. I'm crushed, actually. We were close friends."

Justin's sadness enveloped him and it was difficult to shake off.

Eli said, "She's ready for you, and I'm really sorry as well. It's tough to lose a great friend."

"Thank you both, I appreciate it. Let's go up front so I can catch Bob before you all leave."

The three of them walked the short hallway to the lobby of the mortuary to meet back up with Bob.

"Bob, thanks for everything, I'm grateful for all your help."

They shook hands and nodded at each other with mutual respect and friendship.

"Anytime, Justin. Let me know if there's anything I can do to help you."

"I'll let you know, thanks again."

Bob nodded his head in agreement and the three men left.

Justin turned the open sign to closed and locked up. He wanted to say his goodbyes to Morgan before he left to talk to her parents. Walking back to the cold room, the lights flickered a bit more than they did last time. He opened the door and slowly walked up to Morgan. He pulled the sheet gently down to see her face. He gasped at the sheer horror of seeing the blackened skull with much of the skin burned off. Her eyes were gone, but her teeth remained. It appeared as if she was screaming and in enormous pain when she died. His heart hurt for what she must have experienced. Covering her back up felt more respectful until he had to work on her. He walked over to the thermostat and adjusted the temperature again a couple of degrees colder, just to be sure he preserved her properly.

As he turned back toward Morgan's body, he saw the unthinkable. Slowly, the top half of her body rose and stopped at a sitting position, with the sheet falling, drifting down on her charred thighs. Turning slightly to face him with the missing eyes that felt like they were boring into his soul, the burned body screamed and wailed like the pain she must have really experienced. Justin froze out of sheer terror and began to breathe in short, quick gasps. His skin turned clammy while his heart felt like it was going to break out of his chest. He had a million thoughts run through his head and one of them included getting the fuck out of there. She sighed deeply and fell back down with a thud on the silver table. He rushed over and pushed her into the mortuary cabinet and locked it. Immediately, she began banging around and screaming for a few minutes, not wanting to be trapped. The devil was at work and Justin couldn't escape him, as he was there at every turn, no matter where he went. Feeling defeated, he decided to go home and talk to Morgan's parents in the morning.

Justin was drinking heavily to numb the pain of losing Morgan. He couldn't help but replay every conversation they had to discern if maybe there was someone that would want to hurt her. She kept secrets from her parents and who knows who else. She was comfortable talking to him and he became not only her mentor, but her confidante. Her parents would not have approved of her secret relationship with another young woman. He took them out to lunch or dinner on occasion, and no one suspected anything. They knew in public they had to appear to be just friends, but Justin knew otherwise. He needed to talk to Nicole tomorrow and Morgan's parents both. Nicole may have more insight about what happened since they lived together. He didn't know if Nicole even knew that Morgan was gone, but she was probably contacted by police. Tears streamed down his face as sadness overcame him. He was overwhelmed by everything sinister, disturbing, and heartbreaking that had happened the last couple of days. He poured another double shot of whisky. After he finished his drink, he set the rocks glass down on the coffee table and closed his eyes. He only planned on resting for a short time.

He woke up with his head leaning on the back of the couch, still sitting up like he was the night before. Glancing at the watch still on his wrist, he saw that it was nearly 6:00 in the morning. He knew he had a tough day ahead. The headache he woke up with was a reminder of the night before. Massaging his forehead to lessen the throb, he peered at his phone out of the corner of his eye, since he was getting a phone call. Grunting and feeling dread well up inside, he bit the bullet and answered. It was too late; they had hung up as he answered. Checking his text messages to see if he missed any, he saw that he had missed several from Andy, who also worked for him. He must have gone in early this morning. What happened there flooded his mind again, and he decided to jump in the shower to get ready lightning fast.

Andy was pacing in the lobby when Justin walked in.

"Andy, what is going on?"

"Um, I can't get a hold of Morgan. I think we should call the police!" he said.

"Andy, sit down. We don't need to call the police."

"What the hell are you talking about? She's *missing*!"

"Andy, *please*. Just sit here, right next to me. I know what's going on."

Andy sat down and looked at Justin expectantly. Moving his foot up and down was a coping mechanism so he wouldn't cry. He certainly wanted to keep that a secret. Similar to Morgan, he trained under Justin. He was young, at only twenty-four, and was finishing up his program to become a mortician like Justin. He wanted to work as an apprentice first because his career was everything to him. Morgan was a close friend, as they were the same age and really connected.

With a quivering voice, "Andy, Morgan is in the cooler room in the only occupied locker. I'm so sorry to be the one to tell you. She was murdered and burned alive at the old graveyard."

"What? *No*. This can't be true! *Please* tell me this is just a cruel joke. I can't. I really can't. *This isn't real*." Andy began to sob uncontrollably with his head held in his hands.

Justin sat there, hating every moment and not knowing how to console Andy, who was still stricken with grief. He knew they had become close, and the three of them had an unshakable bond. Being a mortician didn't prepare you for dealing with the grief of the ones left on earth after the dead were gone. There's a class called Funeral Services Psychology and Counseling, where he learned how to talk to the families and loved ones. This is something that is not innate to some, and Justin struggled with empathy for the living.

Andy looked at Justin, waiting for a response. "I want to see her."

"Oh, Andy. I don't think that's a good idea. She's unrecognizable."

"I really get it, but I want to say goodbye before her funeral."

"Only if you promise not to remove the sheet and look at her. I don't want that to be the last time you see her and what you remember, hmm?" said Justin.

"Fine, I agree." Andy got up from his chair with devastation all over his face.

Andy followed Justin to the cold room. Justin's muscles tensed up, his fists were flexing, and his thoughts were on the event last night. Hoping there wouldn't be a repeat, he decided to remain in the room even if Andy asked for privacy. Justin pulled Morgan's drawer out and looked at her quizzically.

"Justin, you looked surprised. Have you not seen her yet?"

"Oh, yeah, I did. It's just difficult to wrap my brain around. I'm staying here in case you need me."

Andy looked at him and silently nodded his head in agreement. He cautiously walked over to Morgan's body and pulled up a stool. He talked to her like she was there in mind and spirit. Justin didn't hover. He was near the embalming table across the room, checking the inventory spreadsheets for the coming week and patiently waiting for Andy to finish. He could hear Andy's sniffles as he scooted the stool back to stand up. Morgan was pushed back into the drawer, and then he locked it. A whisper was barely audible as both were leaving.

Justin, join us.

Andy looked back and was confused. He could have sworn he heard Morgan's voice, but that wasn't possible. He closed the door behind him, shaking with a wild-eyed expression.

"Andy, we should leave early. Let's grab some food and you can go home afterward. I'll keep you posted on what happens with Morgan's parents. Let's go to the diner, my treat."

Andy nodded his head yes. "I'll meet you there."

"No, I'll drive. You shouldn't drive after what you've just been through. Come on. I'll drop you off here to pick up your car when we're done. I won't accept no for an answer."

Andy smiled and slid into the passenger seat of Justin's Mercedes. He loved riding in his car. It was a beautiful sedan. Justin got into the driver's seat and turned the music on, listening to an 80's station. He had Sirius radio, and he listened to mostly hard rock. He figured Andy may not be a fan, so he kept the volume low and the music light.

Driving with the windows down, they let the chilly fall breeze hit their faces, turning their cheeks a slight pink color. As their hair whipped back and forth from the force of the wind tunnel in the car, it alleviated the stress and melted the sadness away, for a moment at least. Halloween was fast approaching and so much sadness and sinister occurrences had hit the town of Stahl with the powerful backhand of an abusive monster. Justin wondered if it was like this every Halloween. *I'll have to get used to it if I survive the season*, he thought. Fall was in full swing with all the vibrant leaves adorning the trees along the highway. Colors of autumn blurred past as he drove to the diner, dreading what was to come after the meal he and Andy would share. His thoughts continued to wander as he drove, arriving at his destination more quickly than he'd expected. Much of the time he was exhausted and experienced highway hypnosis frequently. The diner was located on the outskirts of town. The drive there through town only took about fifteen minutes. When they pulled in it wasn't packed yet. The time was creeping up on 9:00 a.m. Justin pulled in slowly, since the parking lot was gravel and he didn't want to risk scratching his new car.

After they both ordered their food, they shared memories of Morgan while they ate. The meal and spending time together was very therapeutic for the both of them.

"Andy, I'm going to Nicole's after we leave here. Would you like to go?"

"I dunno. You think I should?"

"I think you should do whatever you're comfortable with."

"Alright. I'll go with you. I think it's important to show Nicole we both care and to give her the support that she'll probably need."

"Then it's decided. We both go and brunch is on me. Put your wallet up Andy." Giving him a small smile, Andy complied.

"Thank you." Andy smiled back in return and nodded.

"Looks like dark clouds are rolling in. We should head out soon."

Justin looked a little worried, since he didn't realize it was supposed to storm today. He quickly paid the cashier, and they left. As soon as they both were secure in the car, the clouds opened, and sheets of rain fell upon them.

Three

Driving in torrential rains had proved to be a slow and cautious endeavor. Given the circumstances, it would take twice the time to get to Nicole's house. Justin paced himself well under the speed limit to ensure he arrived at Nicole's safely. He changed the station to something more relaxing, and he only looked down for a few seconds. When he looked back up to focus on the road, the rain had turned to blood.

"What the fuck?" Justin had raised his voice and startled Andy.

"What's wrong?" Andy asked worriedly.

"Don't you *see*?" Justin raised his voice again, only this time, the octave was a couple of notes higher.

"See what, Justin? I don't see anything except the rain." He looked even more worried than a minute ago.

"The rain is now *blood*! How do you *not* see that?" Justin thought he was losing his mind.

"It's just regular rain, Justin. I think your mind is playing tricks on you because you're tired and stressed," Andy tried to reassure him.

Justin blinked a few times, and the rain was once again, just rain. He shook his head in utter disbelief. His thoughts were reeling with why he saw what he did, and Andy didn't. *What is happening to me?* he thought to himself. He had recently been consumed with what was going on and trying to solve the mystery at the graveyard and church.

"You know, you're probably right. I'm just really stressed. I'm sorry, I didn't mean to freak you out." Justin shot Andy a quick glance.

"I think you should probably get to bed early tonight and get some sleep. I can open for you in the morning if you'd like."

"That would be great, thank you. Oh, look, I believe we're here," he said.

They parked in the driveway since there was room, and it was still raining. Justin had two umbrellas in case one broke, so he grabbed them both from the backseat, and handed one to Andy.

"You ready for this?" Justin asked.

"Not really, but we don't have a choice." He took a deep breath and opened the car door to brave the elements with the help of the borrowed umbrella. Justin followed suit and they both were on the porch, knocking on the door after running to escape the rain. After a minute or so, the front door opened.

Nicole looked surprised to see them at the door. "Oh, hi, you two! Morgan isn't here. What can I do for ya?"

"That's why we're here. Can we come in? This might take a while," Justin whispered.

"Oh, sure. Come on. You can sit in the living room. Do you want coffee? I just made a fresh pot. I couldn't sleep last night, and I'm exhausted. I haven't heard from Morgan, and I can't tell you how worried I am."

"We would love a cup of coffee, Nicole, thank you. I take mine with creamer, and Andy, what about you?"

"Just black is fine, thank you." Andy couldn't look Nicole in the eyes when he spoke.

She quietly went into the kitchen and grabbed two cups of coffee and made them as they asked. Her steps were quiet since she had thick fuzzy socks on, which absorbed the sound on the old wooden hardwood floors.

"Here you go." She handed them each their cup and sat down where she had her coffee and book propped on the armrest of her loveseat.

Justin jumped when she spoke because he was lost in thought.

"Nicole, we needed to talk to you about Morgan. We know where she is, but you should, too," Justin said gently.

"Okay, go on," Nicole spoke with trepidation, and her voice quivered.

"Nicole, Morgan was found dead by the old pine tree at the Stahl graveyard. She had been burned to death. We don't know why she was there or who could've done that to her. I know the police are investigating, but I'm surprised that they haven't talked to you yet since you live together." Justin was hoping Nicole could talk about it without falling apart.

"Oh, my God. *No*, no, no, no. How? *Why*? I don't under-stand!" Nicole began to cry hysterically. She held her head in her hands and shook uncontrollably while the tears flowed. Justin jumped up to get her a tissue from the tissue box near him on the end table. He handed one to her and brought the box over. She took the tissue gratefully. Nicole blew her nose and took a few deep breaths so she could talk. She looked up at Justin and Andy.

"I'm so sorry to be the one who had to tell you, Nicole. Truly." While speaking to her gently, Justin sat back down. "Something happened to me at that graveyard, and I told Morgan about it. I'm guessing she went there to see for her-self, but I don't really know. Did she talk to you about it?"

Nicole sighed. "We did talk about it, and I told her not to go because it sounded like things were going on that are otherworldly, if you catch my drift. We got into a fight about it, and she had been staying at her parents' house since then. I guess that's why I haven't heard anything. We didn't break up, it was just a fight, and we were on a short break."

"Did Morgan's parents know about the two of you being a couple? I know they didn't as of about a month ago, but had things changed since then?" Andy asked.

Nicole scoffed, "No. She refused to tell them she was gay. She was so scared that her parents wouldn't love her anymore. Every time she got up the courage and said she was going to tell them, and tell them about *us*, she backed out and remained silent. It's so hard to do that, to tell your parents when they don't know much about that world. The fear of rejection is powerful when you have no idea how your loved ones will react."

"Nicole, I'm so sorry. I'm sure it was difficult to not be open about your relationship and be able to go about your day like you want with the woman you loved," Andy said.

Nicole nodded her head in agreement, and tears welled up and fell again. She grabbed a tissue and gained her composure. Standing up, she walked up to Justin and Andy and hugged them both.

"Thank you both for telling me. Thank you for your friendship, too. I know Morgan loved you both. I'm going to miss our lunches and dinners," Nicole said.

Nicole's sadness was evident with her sagging shoulders and her shaky, quiet voice that was nearly a whisper.

Justin spoke up first, "Our lunches can continue as usual, Nicole. You have an open invitation to go with us when we go, promise."

"Yeah, we would love for you to still meet up with us, you're still our friend," Andy said, while giving her another hug on their way out.

Justin carefully closed the door behind them, and he and Andy left to head over to Morgan's parents' home.

Four

The meeting with Morgan's parents Monday morning went as well as expected. They were heartbroken that she was gone and had no idea of the life she led. It wasn't their place to tell them, so they didn't offer up the truth about Nicole. As far as they knew, Nicole was simply her best friend. Justin helped plan the funeral for Morgan and was only charging a fraction of the cost since Morgan worked for him. Unease grew in his heart as the parents wanted her buried in the Stahl graveyard and not the newer cemetery outside of town. They bought family plots years ago. The funeral was planned for Thursday morning at 10:00.

The last thing Justin wanted to do was worry the Webbers about the funeral, so he kept all the things that had recently occurred to himself. He did wonder if Morgan's soul was in purgatory or heaven. He often wondered if God existed, or just the Devil. Did it have to be both? He wasn't sure what he believed anymore, since exploring the graveyard and church remains. One thing he knew for sure was that the Devil was here in Stahl, and he was dancing on the graves of the loved one's past. Now he was trying to take Justin with him. He needed to get back to his research to figure out how to stop the evil that was oppressive and ominous. The first thing he must do is take care of Morgan and then he could work on the town mystery that everyone was ignoring or unaware of.

After he left the Webbers, he was on the way to his mortuary to begin preparations for Morgan. They wanted her to be cremated since that is what she wanted but the parents wanted to have a service. He had given Andy the day off because he was basically kicked in the teeth for two days straight and he needed time to himself.

Justin turned on the retort to heat up to a toasty 1,500 degrees. It would take a couple of hours to burn Morgan's remains. While he waited the half hour for the chamber to heat up, he plopped down in front of the computer at the desk in his office down the hall. He decided he would finish Morgan's paperwork, then do a little Stahl research. The paperwork for Morgan didn't take long since her parents signed off on everything. They wanted a graveside service at the creepy graveyard. He couldn't talk them out of it since they bought plots there years ago and wanted Morgan's ashes buried there. The graveyard was privately owned, and the owner was not selling new plots due to space.

The whispers he heard about the church ruins and graveyard, combined with what was happening to him, were more than enough reason to see if he could dig into the past of his new hometown. He reread the articles on the Whittier family to see if maybe there was a connection, but he didn't think so. He decided in the morning he would visit the graveyard to investigate again and locate the plot for Morgan, killing two birds with one stone.

Standing up and stretching from his chair, he headed back to the cremation chamber. He had placed Morgan in the wooden container and then secured her in the cremation chamber. In a couple of hours, the process should be complete. He needed coffee, so he went to his office to make a cup from his Keurig. The phone rang before he left his office.

"Hello, this is Justin with York Family Mortuary, how can I be of service?"

All Justin could hear was static, then, *"Justin, we need you."*

Justin quickly hung up the phone. The lights started to flicker like they did last time. A loud buzzing noise could be heard in succession to the lights going off and on. The last thing he needed was for the cremation chamber to lose power. He sighed deeply. An orchestra of disastrous proportions elevated his awareness to his current situation. He was scared to go back to the cremation chamber. With coffee in hand, he decided to brave the short walk there. He did take some comfort in knowing that the back-up generator connected to the cremation chamber would kick in if necessary. To ensure everyone's safety, he would need to call an electrician in the morning. He shut his office door and walked toward the cremation chamber. The lights flickered off for a few seconds.

A shadow was near him and seemed to inch closer by the second. The lights came back on, and he drew in a sharp breath and looked around, but he couldn't see anything out of the ordinary. The lights flickered off again. He was in front of the door to the cremation chamber, and he reached out to touch it. It was ice cold. He quickly drew in his breath and next to him, something breathed out. Justin slowly turned his head, and he locked eyes with something straight from Hell, and it screamed a shrill, drawn-out shriek. As soon as it started, it was over, and the lights returned as if nothing had happened and it was just business as usual. Justin found himself panting out of fear, with clammy shaky hands, and smelled a hint of burning flesh. With a state-of-the-art filtration system, a body couldn't smell while it was burned here. It was something else entirely.

He opened the door and began to move into the room to finish the process of the flame cremation of Morgan. He opened the retort to brush out the remains, and separated the silver medallion with the identification serial number.

Gray ash and bone fragments are what remained, and Justin put them all in a plastic satchel and sealed it. He attached the medallion to the bag so Morgan could be identified, and her parents would be able to take her if they changed their mind about the burial. They had a couple of days. He extended that courtesy since she worked here and he cared about her as a colleague and friend. Typically, there really wasn't a deadline unless the service was scheduled. He could hold on to the remains for months if they needed him to. But, as it turned out, he didn't think he would have to worry about it. He placed the bag in the urn her parents bought. It was beautiful, a Fractured Burning Turn Wood Cremation Urn with blue fractures. He gently placed her bagged remains in the urn, and instead of placing it on the shelf with the others, he took it to his office. It made him feel better about it, and he could talk to her that way. He placed her on his mahogany desk and decided to call it a day; here anyway.

Five

After grabbing some lunch at a local sandwich shop, he decided to drive out to the Stahl graveyard to locate the Webber burial plots and snoop more at the church ruins. He pulled into the isolated tree-lined road with deep, lush, wooded areas on both sides of the road that led up to the graveyard. The gravel crunched under his tires, reminding him to drive slowly. The road before the entrance was covered in potholes that had been patched multiple times; it was like avoiding an infinite number of landmines. Checking his phone was a reminder that service was spotty at best here. He parked at the chain-link gate adorned with a large rusty padlock. He had a key this time from the graveyard owner, so his entrance was much easier.

Walking to the graveyard in a general direction of where he thought the plots would be was peaceful. He heard birds calling to their friends, crickets chirping, and the rustle of branches brushing up against each other as the Kansas wind blew slightly. It had been several days since he felt at peace. This was the first time at the graveyard he'd felt this way. Continuing his walk to the plots, he felt a twinge of something he couldn't quite put his finger on. Lost in thought, he bumped into a headstone. Looking down, it was the Margaret Whittier plot.

Interesting, he thought. No idea if it meant anything, but when he glanced up, he saw the Webber plots. Three in a row. In a few days, Morgan's will be dug up. Her parents placed the order for the headstone already, because sometimes it takes a while to get them in. If nothing else, the Webbers were efficient and timely with handling everything. As he gazed at the plots, his thoughts drifted. A large, cold hand grasped him and his mind was sent to another time.

Several years ago, in 1977, before the church was in ruin, on Emmanuel Hill, it housed evil while the Devil paid a visit. No one knew why he was there, or if they'd live to survive another moment. It was hell on earth, and Stahl was enveloped in darkness on Halloween. Halloween fell on a Sunday that year, and the evening service was cloaked in evil as the Devil made his presence known. The walls bled rivers of blood as numerous members of the congregation had rivulets of blood leak from the corners of their eyes. Screams could be heard for miles as men, women, and children slowly dropped to the floor writhing in excruciating pain. Tears mixed with blood ran down the pastor's face as he watched his congregation suffer at the hands of those whom he had spent a lifetime protecting them from. He stood motionless and helpless. He felt powerless, but all he could think to do was recite Bible verses to protect the people and pray that the Devil grew bored and moved on from Stahl.

Beginning with Psalm 23:4, Pastor Barnes yelled, holding his Bible, "Even though I walk through the valley of the shadow of death, I fear no evil, for You are with me; Your rod and Your staff, they comfort me." Reciting this from memory as his eyes were closed, and still, blood flowed from them. He remained faithful and strong for his congregation and kept reciting the same verse over and over again.

"Foolish Pastor. That will not make me leave." His laughter bellowed and reverberated throughout the church while the people still suffered, crying and moaning in pain.

"No, but I draw strength from Him by showing my devotion for as long as I can."

Laughing, the Devil spoke to him in a condescending tone. "Pastor, I pity you. You follow a nobody who will do nothing for you. I can give you everything you desire. What would you like?" He waited for a reply.

He stayed in the shadows so Pastor Barnes couldn't see his face. The pastor could see the massive horns on his head, his glowing, sharp yellow teeth, and elongated fingers with pointed black nails. They were reminder enough of the urgency of him remaining faithful and strong.

"There is nothing you can give me that I want. I have every- thing I need." Pastor Barnes spoke with conviction.

"Oh? Is that so? What about Lillie Robenson? Remember her and how you craved her in every sinful way possible? Those lonely nights you burned with desire for her, but all you had for pleasure was yourself? Remember? Because I do..."

"Shut up, Devil!" Pastor Barnes roared at the vile but truthful words spoken out loud in front of his congregation.

He was divorced at the time, but she was married. He did yearn for her, but she moved away, and they lost touch. Hoping no one noticed their battle of words, or heard the actual words spoken, he prayed. He was fighting for them, but his soul felt weakened by the Devil.

Justin felt the cold hand squeeze his own firmly, and then slowly let go. He opened his eyes and looked around. His thoughts flooded to the vision he was shown. He felt like now there were multiple spirits at war, and he was caught in the middle. The frigid hand seemed to want to show him the battle between the pastor and the Devil. At least he had a direction for his research. Pastor Barnes and Lillie Robenson might be the lead he needed to find out what this spirit wanted him to know.

"Who are you? Why are you showing me these visions?" Justin whispered and hoped for a response, but he knew he wouldn't get one.

Justin walked up the short hill to the church ruins. He was walking around, looking for the spiral staircase to the basement, when he noticed a home in the near distance on the other side of the corn field. He noticed neither before. The dilapidated two-story house with multiple windows was glowing red from the inside. It seemed odd. He ventured into the corn field and gently knocked the corn stalks out of the way as he moved toward the direction of the home. The closer he got, the further away it seemed. He was growing thirsty as he continued, and he thought he should abandon the crazy idea to go to a home where he knew no one and could encounter something dangerous.

He turned around to go back toward the church and would see if there was a road that led to the home later. As he began to walk back, he heard the crunching of corn stalks. He hoped it was just a harmless animal, but he picked up his pace, nonetheless. The goal was to get home as soon as possible. He looked up to see the sky darkening above him. It's as if darkness was following him and was about to unleash buckets of rain with a little bit of thunder and lightning for good measure. He could hear the rustling of cornstalks and rumbling in the distance. His heart matched the quick glide of his footfalls. He was now running, yet time seemed to slow down here. He stumbled into a clearing by the church and had never been happier to see it. Muffled growling could be heard in the distance. He didn't feel like sticking around to see what was behind him. He ran to his car to head home as exploring the church would have to wait for another time. Before he jumped in his car after he secured the padlock on the gate, he noticed the black SUV that had previously followed him.

Sighing with disdain, he went up to the SUV and knocked on the tinted driver's side window. It slid down and the same man he had dealt with before was the face that stared back at him.

"I have permission to be here. There will be a family here for a service this week. I was checking on the location of the family plots." Justin felt like he needed to defend himself.

"That's why you were playing in the corn stalks, huh?" The man spoke with sarcasm dripping from every word.

Justin just looked at him and shook his head. "You don't know what you're talking about. And stop following me."

"You know, Justin, I'm trying to keep you alive, but you're making it difficult." He rolled the window back up and drove off slowly, watching Justin in his rearview mirror. Tired,

Justin decided to go home. He would handle the things tomorrow that he didn't get done today.

Six

Justin knew he wouldn't be able to sleep just yet, so he thought he'd stay up late and organize parts of the house he hadn't gotten to yet. Several boxes remained in the basement. He had plans of finishing out the basement as an additional living space with a den, bathroom, and full bar. But first, he should unpack the boxes for his office library room. He walked over to the corner of the room with his boxes and grabbed a box of books to take upstairs. As he was about to walk the short trek up the stairs, the lights started to flicker like they did at his mortuary.

"What the fuck? *My house too?*" Justin was getting tired of this stuff. He just wanted a normal life.

In the opposite corner of the basement the shadow emerged slightly as the lights continued to flicker. He couldn't tell who the shadow belonged to, but his flesh prickled with fear, and he caught his breath. The outline of the shadow gave likeness to a man, or, more likely something that wasn't quite human. Shadows encompassed all corners of the basement. Cobwebs and dust filled all corners except the one near the stairs, where the stack of boxes sat. The concrete floor was several layers deep with dirt and the dust on the concrete walls mingled with deathwatch beetles. The only light source was a singular dull light bulb with a long pull chain.

"Who's there? Show yourself. I'm tired of you hiding from me." Justin was so terrified, he was surprised he could put together a coherent sentence.

Whispering, the shadow answered, "Who I am does not matter, we want you to join us, *just join us*..." Its voice trailed off, and the shadow dissipated with the beetles.

The light came back on, and Justin grabbed the one box. He moved upstairs quicker than he thought possible. He took the box to his office and library room and set it down on his desk. Sighing deeply, he realized that no matter where he went, the shadow followed him. He decided to work on getting the books in the built-ins and just bury himself in the work of getting his home in order. After he finished one box, he went to get a second. The basement was quiet, and no sinister shadows were wreaking havoc in Justin's imagination or in the basement. He decided to just bring them all up and set them just outside the basement door. Five boxes later, he felt like that was enough for the evening. The basement door shut on its own; he looked back and shivered. After he carried the five boxes to his office, he breathed deeply to calm down. Staring at his bookshelves, he decided to put the books in alphabetical order by author last name and by genre. He felt that was the easiest way to find what he needed. Two hours later, he had made a significant dent in his bookshelves being finished. He wasn't a fan of knickknacks or tchotchkes, but he may add a plant or two to the bookshelves instead. He loved bringing the outdoors inside. After he broke down the boxes, he stacked them in the corner to take to recycling later. He cleaned off his new beautiful mahogany desk. Truth be told, he'd always had an affinity for dark wood. He felt it was classier than any other variation. He set up his laptop, his pens, the little cactus plant he bought for his desk, and connected the computer to the printer he'd already set up. He felt good about the progress he'd made, so he was calling it a night.

Heading to his kitchen, he thought he would open a bottle of red wine. He loved Vampire wine and ordered a case of the cabernet recently. Pouring generously into his wine glass, he went to relax in his living room. Setting his wine down, he pulled out a vinyl record of Hall & Oates and placed it on his turntable. A guilty pleasure of his was to sit on the couch to enjoy the music and wine he needed to relax; the simple things in life were good for his spirit. Sipping the wine and singing along with the record provided a distraction from the shadow. Somehow, he knew that the shadow needed to gain his attention, if only briefly. The record slowed down, and the lyrics nearly sounded demonic. Justin stopped, set his wine down, and looked at his turntable. It looked as if it was melting, which he thought probably explained the change in the speed of the music. He got up to look at it closer and it was normal again. He scratched his head in confusion and went back to the couch to have a seat. Grabbing his wine again, he swallowed the rest of it quickly and decided he needed to get some sleep. He washed down some sleeping pills so he could have uninterrupted rest.

Waking up after getting the best sleep he'd had in some time, Justin woke to darkness in his bedroom and shadows populating his room. He peered over at the analog clock and saw it was shortly after 7:00 am; the sun should be shining through the blinds in streams of light, welcoming him to the day. Instead, he was in complete darkness. His heart began to pound harder than a whore who was earning her hour of work. Shadows shifted at a steady pace toward him—at least three. The melodic whispers in a repetitive chant were difficult to interpret, and he didn't try due to being terrified and catatonic against his will. His immobility was at the hands of the shadows that he couldn't escape from. All he could do was hope he wouldn't die, or maybe by the time it was over, he'd want to die.

The chanting whispers were so close he could feel the breeze from their words. He began to get hot. Sweat beads formed above his lips and on his forehead. His breath became short, and breathing was difficult. He still couldn't get out of his bed or move at all. The shadow dipped in and out of Justin's body, causing him to have convulsions. His eyes rolled into the back of his head as he shook violently. After a few minutes of the shadow moving through Justin's body like he belonged to it, it finally stopped. Disappearing at once, the room became light again after the shadows left. The sun was streaming through the blinds like it normally would and Justin was groggy, but awake. Getting a grip of his bearings, he looked around and looked at the clock. Losing thirty minutes where he wasn't sure what happened, and time that he couldn't get back, was disturbing. He was bothered by not knowing. He slowly sat up on the edge of his bed. Stretching and scratching his head, he looked behind him and noticed the sweaty sheets and pillowcases.

"Gross, guess I'm doing laundry." He looked at his bed with utter disgust, as he didn't normally sweat when he slept, since he ran a fan on himself and kept his home at 68°.

Slowly standing up, he steadied himself with the mattress, stripped the bed, and then went to the bathroom to shower and get ready for the day.

Feeling better after the shower, he quickly dressed, grabbed the sheets, and went to the laundry room down the hall to drop the sheets in the washer. Desperate for coffee, he went to make a strong cup and read the news on his computer in his office. He pulled his favorite coffee cup from the cabinet and waited for the coffee to finish brewing. He turned on the mini TV next to his coffee maker to pass the time before he got settled in his office. The news was typical, with local events, the weather, and the recent deaths made Justin ponder if that was normal here. He turned up the volume to hear it better. Someone had died in their sleep after briefly waking up and something scared them, literally to death. It wasn't someone he knew, but their wife recounted the events for the police. A neighbor called the police when they heard his wife screaming. This was concerning because he felt like something similar happened to him, but he was lucky that he didn't die from it. Pouring his coffee and turning off the TV, he decided that he had enough of the news and opted to work on paperwork in his office until he got the call about the newly deceased.

Wrapping up the paperwork for the morning was a good feeling. He was all caught up. Tomorrow was Morgan's service, so he needed to call her parents to ensure everything was still a go and to see if they needed anything in general.

"Mrs. Webber. Yes, It's Justin. Just checking in. I wanted to make sure that there weren't any changes to the service. Great, sounds good. Hey, Mrs. Webber, I'm going to be in the area later, do you two need anything? I'm happy to pick up some things at the store for you. Okay, just thought I'd offer. You're very welcome. Yes, see you tomorrow."

Justin clicked off with the red "end call" button and set his phone down on his desk. Polishing off his black coffee in one giant gulp, he stood up. Suddenly he felt dizzy and sat back down. Guessing he got up too quickly, he tried it again. More slowly this time, he stood up and stood still for a minute. He felt okay and decided to head to the couch for a bit and relax. He was overcome with a feeling of nausea. He laid down and turned the TV on to watch a movie. He needed something mindless. There was a stupid horror movie on Netflix, called *Killer Sofa*, and he settled on that. He watched about two minutes of it and decided it wasn't for him. He channel surfed until he landed on *Top Gun*. That was a great movie. Closing his eyes, he dozed off. Two hours later he woke up.

"What the hell?" Justin said as he looked at his phone and realized that he had slept for quite a while, when he didn't intend on sleeping at all. Now, it was nearly 11:00 a.m. and he had numerous missed calls. Andy had called him several times, so he quickly got up and grabbed his keys and his wallet and headed out the door.

Andy met Justin at the door. His face was scrunched up and he was wringing his hands, which was how Justin knew he was stressed.

"I'm so sorry, Andy. I haven't been feeling well and accidentally took a nap. What did I miss?"

"Well, did you hear of that guy who died in his sleep? His wife came in and wanted to talk to you. I tried to handle things, but she refused. She said she would only talk to you because you were more like *her*. I got the feeling that she wouldn't talk to me because I'm black. I'm so sorry, I tried to get started on it, but she wouldn't let me. She wasn't very nice at all. She is all yours, man!" Andy shrugged, indicating he had tried, but to no avail; she wasn't having it.

"You mean to tell me she wouldn't let you handle *anything*? What an old twat. I'll call her and under no certain terms is she to defer to me if you are here. That's fucking ridiculous! Did she at least leave her phone number? I'll be happy to mention also that I will either sell or leave this business to you before anyone else on this earth. She needs to know you're my right hand. By the way, I'm giving you a raise. You have gone above and beyond since we lost Morgan. You're now salaried and full-time, with benefits. Every year your salary will include a 5% increase. Sounds good?"

Andy's mouth gaped open like a fish out of water and he quickly pulled himself together. "I think if I can have a yearly 6% raise, we can shake on it."

Justin gave Andy a smile that grew and held out his hand. "Sir, you drive a hard bargain, but we have a deal. I'll draw up the paperwork this week."

They shook hands and Andy had never felt more happiness and pride than he did at that moment. It nearly made up for the ridiculousness of the old lady.

Justin went to his office to call the old curmudgeon and yelled out to Andy, "Hey Andy, I'm gonna make that dreadful phone call, so you're in charge until I come up for air!"

"Sounds good, thanks boss!" Andy sat at the desk in the foyer of the mortuary.

Andy knew this mortuary was nicer than most he had interviewed with last year, in surrounding towns. He was so grateful he made the right choice. On the books, the schedule didn't seem to have anything listed. He looked at the schedule again on the desktop to see if there were any appointments he missed, but nothing appeared for today. But, that could always change at a moment's notice with a phone call.

Deep in thought about his graduation and upcoming tests, December was fast approaching. Upon completion of his degree in mortuary science and the passing of his boards in March, that would be the new beginning he dreamed of. At least if he bombed the exam, he could take it again after thirty days. Even though that wouldn't be ideal, at least it was an option. Studying for it in December after he graduated would give him three months, but he'd start studying now to play it safe. He was excited to move forward in his career and be an official funeral director like Justin. Mentoring seemed to be a gift that Justin possessed. Now, if he could only have a social life, that would be awesome. He still hadn't met anyone, as the career he chose, isn't one running rampant with women. Getting out and doing fun things needed to be a priority in the near future. The time spent with Morgan was priceless, and they were with each other most of the time and had an unshakable bond. He missed her more than he could ever convey. He needed to stay busy, so he thought he would start going to the few places in town where he could meet people his age. The library wasn't enough. There was a dive bar, a good restaurant in town, and a small, beautiful park with a pond and benches overlooking a grove of trees near the creepy Stahl graveyard. This town was so small, *you blink you miss it,* he thought. He had grown to love it though.

"Andy? You up front?" Justin yelled out.

"Yeah boss, still here!"

"Good. Let's go to lunch. Grab anything you need; we're having a working lunch."

They both walked out of the mortuary and jumped into Justin's car.

After lunch, Justin and Andy discussed business. Justin went over several of the daily tasks that Andy had not had to do before. Little did Andy know, Justin wanted him able to run the mortuary with success if something happened to him. He had a gut feeling that he may be at risk of not being around anymore, considering all the things that had happened recently.

"So tomorrow morning, I want you to open and do the things we discussed, Andy. Can you manage that? If you need me to shadow you, I can."

"No, I think I got it. I have my notes here too. I'll go over them again tonight and in the morning before work. Thanks again Justin, I really do appreciate the opportunity to make you proud and to be your right hand man."

Justin adored the guy and appreciated his enthusiasm. He just hoped after tomorrow he was ready. He'd draw up the papers for him to inherit the business upon his untimely death and the salary increase contract.

"Well, I have set old lady Donaldson straight. She knows that I won't tolerate that bigoted behavior and she will deal with us *both*. She is using the newer cemetery in town for the burial. She purchased a plot for herself too. She just wants a short and sweet graveside service since they don't have any family, and they never had kids. Not much to do in that way. The body should arrive later this afternoon and the funeral is set for next Monday."

"Thank you, I appreciate you talking to her. Hopefully, any interactions moving forward will be positive ones."

"If they aren't, you let me know. I'll tell her I'll just roll her in a hole and throw dirt on her when she dies if she can't behave." Justin chuckled and Andy joined him.

They needed the bonding time and release of all the tension they had been holding in. However brief it may be, laughter was good for their souls. As things were about to get dark, the souls of Stahl were at risk. Justin had more detective work to do, so after he dropped Andy off at the mortuary, he planned on going back to the graveyard to investigate the church ruins again. Hopefully this time, he would be able to stay and snoop around the church to find the basement stairs again.

"Andy, you ready?"

"Yeah boss, let's go."

"You don't need to call me boss. Please call me Justin, Andy. I promise it's fine. It can be endearing, but I think of you as a colleague, not as your superior. Okay?"

"Absolutely boss...Justin, I mean."

Justin smiled at him, paid the bill, and patted him on the back.

"Ready to go? I have some errands to run," Justin asked Andy.

"Yeah, I'm tired, but I'll be happy to stay at the mortuary if you need me to?"

"No, it's locked up and if anyone needs us, I'll let you know. Take the night off. You deserve it."

"Thank you, I just want to go home and watch movies and eat junk for dinner later."

"Sounds like a great plan."

Getting in Justin's car, they headed back to the mortuary. The fall colors from the trees and bushes they passed by on the short drive were mesmerizing. All the gold, red, and orange leaves were stunning to see, and they usually were gone much too quickly. Justin tended to enjoy the little things in life. He knew how fleeting it could be. Seeing the beauty become a blur as he drove by the wooded areas in town, he became apprehensive thinking about how it would feel if he was never able to see the things he loved and appreciated ever again.

Pulling into the parking lot, he stopped by Andy's car to let him out, and they exchanged their goodbyes for the evening and mentioned they would see each other in the morning. He watched Andy drive off and then he headed to the graveyard and church. Checking to make sure he wasn't being followed

again before he pulled out of the parking lot; he wanted assurance he could stay out there as long as he needed

Seven

By the time Justin arrived at the Stahl Graveyard, it was nearly 2:00 p.m. Plenty of daylight was left to do some of his own investigating. The warm sun hit Justin's face as soon as he stepped out of his car. It was unseasonably warm for the tail end of October. Not a cloud in the sky could be seen for miles. A slight Kansas wind was blowing due East. The crisp autumn air had a certain smell, like a campfire burning charred meat. Leaves blew around from the maple trees and the branches were rubbing against each other creating a rustling sound. The giant pine tree loomed over the crumbling old tombstones and waved to him to pay a visit. Walking over there first before he headed to the church proved to be a distraction, but he thought he had the time. As he neared the pine tree, he smelled burning flesh. Looking around, he didn't notice anything out of the ordinary. When he glanced back to the pine tree, he saw a woman burned beyond recognition, slightly swinging from the hanging branch. He wasn't sure if it was reality or not. Everything was blurred now. This reminded him of what he saw in his nightmare recently.

Horrified at what he was seeing right in front of his face, the burned body turned its head slightly and whispered, *Justin, join us.*

He shook his head back and forth in an attempt to unsee what he viewed or in hopes of it all disappearing. It didn't. It swayed slowly in rhythm to the wind as if they were joined in secrets only they knew, but wanted Justin in on them as well. Justin turned his back to the tree and rushed up to the church ruins. When he got there, he moved around one of the remaining walls that blocked his view of the large pine tree where the evil undead swung. Leaning against the wall, he tried to catch his breath. Glancing at his cell phone, it looked like he had enough battery life to use the flashlight for a while as he looked around. Peeking around the wall to check the tree, he saw the burned ghost woman was gone.

He backed up from the wall and tripped on a few bricks he didn't notice. He stumbled back and fell into the spiral staircase of the basement of the church that had not been sealed off. Losing his grip on the top step, he dangled toward the shadows and the unknown. Damp with sweat, his fingers were slowly sliding off the top step of the winding staircase known to lead to a gateway to Hell. His heartbeat increased with each finger that slipped off. The last two fingers turned white as Justin tried with everything he had to cling to the step, to no avail. He lost the fight and tumbled down, hitting the steps as he descended further and further below the surface.

As he neared the end of his descent, his right foot caught on the last rung of the staircase, which hovered above the concrete. Blood was rushing to his head as he dangled close to the dirty floor. He lifted his upper body to free himself, but it took three tries before he was successful. He bumped into the floor in record speed and knocked the wind out of himself. It took several minutes to get oriented to his surroundings. The spiral staircase fell apart and broke into hundreds of pieces around him as he protected his head and curled into a ball hoping to prevent any serious injuries. After the last bit of staircase hit the floor, he began to look for his phone. Feeling around for his cell phone, he realized that it was his only connection to the outside world. Slowly sitting up, he began to feel around the floor in complete darkness. His eyes weren't adjusting very well and fortunately, some of the things he touched were just small rocks, bricks, and dirt. As he was continuing his blind search, he finally found his phone. He touched it and it lit up the room right around him, but not beyond his reach.

Not knowing what lurked in the darkness gnawed at his consciousness, and he was on high alert. Justin tried to make a phone call to Andy, but there wasn't working cell service in the basement. Growing more concerned by the minute, he began pacing, using the flashlight from his phone. Stupidly, he didn't tell anyone where he was going. No one would think to look down here for him. He tried calling Andy again, and the call still wouldn't go through.

"Fuck!" Justin was frustrated and at a loss as to what to do.

As Justin was considering some options, he leaned against a wall for support. After he put his weight against it, it shifted. Turning around, Justin started to touch the wall in numerous places to see if it would move again. He pushed against it as hard as he could with his hands, and the door was slightly ajar while dust clouds surrounded him. Coughing from getting dust in his mouth, he peeked into the sliver of blackness using his cell phone for light. He couldn't see anything, but he felt a deep, uncontrollable desire to explore and leave all his senses behind.

The old door creaked as he opened it as far as he could push it. The iPhone flashlight wasn't very strong, but it was the only light source that he had. Slowly emerging from one dark room into another, he moved his phone over the walls and the floor as he inched along at a snail's pace. The floor seemed completely intact, so he focused his time exploring the walls for something. He wasn't sure what he was looking for, but he happened upon another secret door. On the door was a lion knocker with a lion's snarling mouth and sharp teeth. Brushing off the years of collected dust, he could see the knocker was bronze and the teeth appeared to be ivory. Haunting yet beautiful, Justin was mesmerized and drawn to it. He needed a photo of it to refer to later. After he took the photo, he pressed down as hard as he could until he could hear the door trying to open. He repeated it multiple times and finally was able to get inside.

A weak light filtered through, hitting Justin in the face. Sighing with relief, he was hopeful this was a way out. Before he reached the light, on the floor was an open hole that led to an even further underground abyss. He laid flat to peer down into the depths of the black hole. Burning fire from a distance was barely visible to the naked eye, but he could see it. That had to be the gateway to Hell he had heard about.

"Unbelievable, that this shit exists," Justin muttered quietly to himself.

This would explain where the shadow had come from. Walking toward the light, he realized that it narrowed slightly, and he could see a ladder to climb up to the light source. Noticing something off to the side in his peripheral vision, he aimed the light from his phone toward what caught his attention. There was a lump of something against the wall, so he moved closer to it. Crouching down, he put his hands on whatever it was and felt it. Covered in a blanket, he felt something crumble a little underneath his touch. Pulling back the dirty blanket, he saw a face staring back at him. Fear caught him by surprise, and he gasped. The skeleton looked so old he felt guilty for desecrating its final resting place. Stumbling back, he caught his fall this time, on the nearby wall. He hurried to the ladder and ascended toward the light, climbing as quickly and carefully as he could. The opening wasn't blocked by anything, so he was able to easily climb out. In front of him was the house he tried to get to recently. Red lights glowed from the windows, giving it an eerie appearance. He decided to go and knock on the door, not able to delay his curiosity any further.

Landing three consecutive, assertive knocks on the door, he waited for someone to open it. No one could be heard moving around from the inside, and no cars were in the driveway. The internal lights still had a red hue from the outside. He waited for a few more minutes, but it was clear that if someone were home, they had no interest in answering the door to a complete stranger. Disappointed, he walked back toward the graveyard to head home. It had been quite the day. As he walked down the hill, he noticed the clouds moving in at a rapid pace. The sun was covered by the storm clouds, darkening his walk to his car. Threatening rain any minute, the skies appeared to be taunting him with the possibility of a downpour. He could only hope that it would hold off at least until he collapsed into his car.

Whispers could be heard in the graveyard as he stepped through the heart of the headstones. Voices became louder, and the chanting, *Join us*, was relentless in his mind. A loud crack of thunder erupted from the sky and lightning struck the roots of the pine tree. A fire was ignited as the burned woman who spoke to Justin earlier was once again swinging dead from the hanging branch. The voices were all-consuming, and Justin stood there in the pouring rain, as his eyes rolled into the back of his head and he dropped to the ground in convulsions. Justin's thoughts were convoluted with the devil taking up residence in his mind, and it was a painful experience.

"Help, please help me, anyone?" Justin pleaded to no one. He was alone, as not another soul visible to the living could be seen.

No longer able to struggle due to being tired and weak, Justin stilled. The rain pelted him as he lay motionless on the ground, with the rain soaking his clothes and cooling his body. As the evening wore on, he remained on the ground, unconscious, as the storm moved on. The pine tree was no longer on fire, and the burned woman was gone as well.

Shadows crept in as darkness claimed the light. Following Justin's every move for the last several days, the large shadow stood near Justin's body. Nudging Justin to wake up, he remained until Justin stirred.

"What's going on? Where am I? Why am I so *cold*?" Justin asked groggily, and slowly opened his eyes. Sitting up, he looked around and realized that he'd never left the graveyard.

What the fuck? he thought.

After carefully standing up, he realized the rain-soaked clothes and shoes made it extremely uncomfortable to walk. His shoes sloshed as he walked the short distance back to his car. He grabbed a dirty towel he had left in his car to sit on while he drove home. He felt grateful he woke up when he did so he could get home. Looking at his phone, he was fortunate that the waterproof case did its job. He missed a few calls from Andy. He would have to call him back after he got home. Starting the car and pulling out onto the road was the easiest part of his evening ahead.

Pulling into his driveway and simultaneously opening the garage, he sighed with relief that he was finally home. The rain had moved through town already, so he didn't have to worry about the rain, not that it mattered. Once he had time to organize his garage, he could park there. He needed to do that soon, before winter arrived.

Justin, we need to talk and there are a few ground rules we need to work through. You are mine now. The shadow whispered to Justin from the backseat.

Justin looked in the rearview mirror and jerked in a combination of surprise and fear.

"Who are you?" Justin asked, with a quivering voice.

I'm what most people question actually exists. I'm here for a reason and I need you.

The shadow spoke with authority, as if Justin could not refuse.

"What do you need me for?" Justin asked.

You'll find out soon enough. Look, there's a black SUV parked across the street. He is following you again. You want me to get rid of him for you? Just say the word and I can make it happen, the shadow said with the utmost confidence.

"You're gonna just tell him to leave? Just like that and he won't follow me again?"

If that is what you'd like, yes. I can do that.

The shadow dissipated from the backseat and moved to the driver's side door of the SUV. The driver immediately put the car in gear and peeled out, leaving both dust and the shadow in his wake.

Justin quickly got out of the car and ran inside the garage, where it was already open. He ran to the kitchen door where the garage access was located and shut the garage, locked the kitchen door, and ran through the house making sure there was no possibility for anyone to get in, not thinking that the shadow wasn't human and barriers meant nothing.

After Justin's shower, he put on dry clean clothes quickly so he could call Andy as he headed to the kitchen to fix himself a quick dinner: a microwaved meal and an apple. He poured himself a glass of wine first and decided to not be sophisticated and sip. He gulped. Pouring more wine in his glass and sitting down with his lackluster meal, he ate faster than usual so he could make the phone call that would likely complicate his evening.

"Andy, what's going on and how can I help?"

"Just wanted to make sure that everything is ready to go for Morgan's service, since her parents called to check. I told them it was, and everything had fallen into place and there was nothing to worry about. Is that okay that I told them that?"

"Andy, that was perfect, thank you. Yes, everything is in order for the service on Thursday."

"Okay, sounds good. Hey, Justin? Is everything alright? You sound strange, like you're worried about something, and I haven't heard you sound like that before." Andy tried to hide his fear that was bubbling to the surface.

"I'm not sure how to answer that. I'm worried about some things, but not work. I seem to be losing time here and there and I can't figure out what's going on. I'm not sure if it's a midlife crisis, or if there are supernatural elements at play that are messing with me. I know how absolutely crazy that sounds, but there are definitely things that have happened that I cannot explain. Things that I think relates to my research on figuring out the past to the graveyard and the church. You want in on the research?"

Laughing nervously, Andy paused for a moment before he responded. "That's not exactly the response I expected, but I can help, sure."

"Look, Andy I know how it all sounds, but earlier today I went to explore the graveyard and church. Something happened and some of it, well most it, I really can't explain, not yet anyway. I woke up on the ground after the storm and I guess I was unconscious, but I don't remember why. After I woke up, I was soaked from the rain and had zero memory of why I didn't get in my car and leave."

"I'm coming over to keep you company. I'll bring a bottle of cab, and we'll hash this all out. Be there in like fifteen." Andy hung up.

Justin cleaned up his dinner and set out another wine glass, then pulled the wine key from the silverware drawer. He poured the last of the wine from his opened bottle into his glass and went to relax in the living room. The TV remote was within reach. Justin grabbed it to mindlessly watch something until Andy arrived. Lights from the street shone through the window behind the couch Justin was sitting on. He turned and pulled the curtains aside to peer outside, where Andy was walking up to the front door. Getting up to answer the door, like clockwork Andy arrived on time.

"Hey Andy, thanks for coming over and bringing the wine. The wine glass and the wine key are on the counter in the kitchen, help yourself."

"Sure thing. Mondavi okay?" Andy wasn't positive if Justin would drink it.

"Absolutely, thanks again."

Andy brought the wine bottle with him and the men descended on the couch at opposite ends and set their wine glasses down. Andy looked expectantly at Justin to fill him in on what he needed to tell him, so what he shared earlier made more sense.

"Andy, as you know, there have been strange events happening over the last several days."

"Justin, I know something weird is going on, I've seen some of it. I need you to tell me what it means and what you're trying to figure out."

"I'm trying to put pieces together of some history of Stahl and figure out exactly what happened to the people buried there from hundreds of years ago. I found something in the church, too. I found a place underground that was a type of basement. I literally tripped and fell into it. Multiple rooms, a skeleton, tunnels, and a gateway to Hell that leads to the house on the hill! I'm sure there are other things there that I didn't get a chance to explore since I was alone and only had the light from my cell phone. But Andy, I'm telling you, there is so much more going on that I just can't figure out. *Fuck, fuck, fuck! Why is this happening?*"

"Okay, that is a lot to...you know, for me to um, take in. That's really a bunch of nonsense, Justin! Seriously? Tell me you are joking? What things have you seen that you don't really understand? Because I can tell you, I don't understand either!"

"A burning pine tree, a burning woman, Morgan sitting up and speaking after she was dead, a shadow man that keeps bothering me and speaking to me. All of these ghosts or entities all have one specific thing they say to me. *Join us.* It's unnerving and I don't know what they want me to join them for, you know? And I seem to randomly lose consciousness now! Nothing about this is *remotely* normal." Justin seemed stressed and mindlessly drank his wine while waiting for Andy to speak.

"Well that's a lot for you to be going through for sure. I can help you with research if you'd like? I don't think you're crazy and I believe there are, um...crazy things at play here. I've heard a lot of stuff, so I think at least some of the things I've heard could have some truth to them," Andy said.

Andy got up to get more wine since he polished his off rather quickly.

"Justin, do you want more wine?"

"No, but can you grab my water from the fridge for me?"

"Sure can," Andy said.

Justin's head was swimming from all the wine he had. By this time the sun had set and the shadows grew outside while the porch automatic light kicked on; he was feeling calmer than he had in hours. Closing his eyes briefly, he started to replay the day in his mind, and he definitely didn't want to do that. He opened his eyes to Andy standing in front of him, holding the chilled Yeti water bottle out for him.

"Justin, you still want your water?"

Looking at Andy with a blank stare, he blinked a few times then recognition registered.

"Yeah, sorry. Thank you." Justin grabbed the bottle of water and took several long gulps, then set it down on the coffee table.

They both talked about what the rest of the work week looked like for them. Andy agreed to open in the morning to give Justin time to rest, and he said he would research the historical significance of Stahl and reach out to his buddy who was a history buff. Andy assured Justin that his friend was trustworthy and wouldn't talk about what he would find. He would give him a call in the morning during the down time at work. During their conversation, a large shadow moved across the windows behind them. They both halted their conversation and watched as their fear built, and they both scrambled to get off the couch and move away as quickly as they could. They watched in horror as the shadow pulled itself off the blinds behind the couch and stood there in the living room with them.

Whispering to Justin, Andy said, "We should go. My keys are in my pocket. Let's slowly head toward the door."

Never taking their eyes off the shadow, they moved toward the front door. Andy opened the door and walked out. When it was Justin's turn, the door slammed shut and he couldn't open it. He kept pulling on the door to leave, but it wouldn't budge. All the lights went out in the house. The shadow moved closer to him, and they were face to face, but in complete darkness he couldn't see features on the shadow.

Time is running out, Justin. You need to join us, it's the only way. The shadow sounded convincing.

"I have no idea what you're talking about," Justin said.

You will, very soon, the shadow whispered.

The shadow moved through Justin and then disappeared into thin air.

"Ugh!" Justin felt like he'd been gut punched. He bent over, holding his stomach, wincing.

Banging could be heard at the front door. Justin stood up straight and cautiously went to answer the door. He unlocked it, opened it, and Andy was there with concern and worry etched across his face.

"What the hell was that, Justin?"

"The shadow man that won't leave me alone."

"Why don't you stay the night with me tonight?" Andy offered.

"Oh, I wish, but it's best if I don't. It's safer for you if I stay here. You should get home and get some rest since you're opening in the morning." Justin's exhaustion was evident as he spoke.

"Justin, you sure? I'm worried about you."

"Yes, of course, go on now. I'll see you in the late morning."

Justin closed the door and locked it after he finally got Andy to leave. He really didn't know what to do with himself now, considering the events of the day. He walked back to the living room and plopped down on the couch, kicked off his shoes, and turned on the TV. Shortly after, he was drifting off to sleep and his eyes moved rapidly indicating he was in a dream state. The shadow reappeared in Justin's dream and sat next to him on the couch while he placed one of his clawed hands firmly over his heart. He whispered in Justin's ear, *join us and I'll show you why.* The shadow placed his other clawed hand over Justin's forehead.

The shadow eased Justin underneath the pine tree in the grave-yard. It was cool in the darkness as the pine tree's branches waved in the breeze while several brown needles fell to the ground where a bed of needles already lay. The dirt was cool and slightly damp from the rains earlier. The uncut grass provided privacy, as Justin couldn't be seen from the rural road near the graveyard. Most people were too scared to venture out here late at night with all the rumors and legends that could possibly ring true. Not many were willing to take that kind of risk.

The shadow looked at Justin like he was his long-lost pet. De-ciding it was time, he placed his hands on Justin's temples. Show-ing him memories from centuries ago, the shadow watched Justin slightly convulse as he convoluted his mind with memories of Stahl from years past. After the sharing of memories was complete, the shadow used Justin's body to test the waters to see if his body was strong enough for the shadow to use him as a conduit, or host. The shadow slipped into Justin's body, but Justin was beginning to have seizures from the unknown entity that decided to take up residency in his body. The shadow needed him alive, so he removed himself and lay next to him on the ground for a moment.

On the couch, Justin stirred and then opened his eyes. He searched for his phone to check the time, and it was 3:13 a.m. He didn't mean to fall asleep on the couch; now he felt like he hadn't really slept at all. Rising from the couch, he noticed some dirt on his clothes, and the back of his shirt was damp. He was confused as to why his clothes were so dirty. He was beginning to remember blips from his dream, but putting that together now, as tired as he was, wasn't going to happen. Pulling off his shirt as he went upstairs, he finished changing clothes and tried to get some sleep.

After Justin got in bed, he turned the lights out, turned the fan on, and relaxed as much as he could so he could drift off. In about twenty minutes he was snoring, and it was nearly 4:00 a.m. The temperature dropped nearly thirty degrees in his bedroom. Dreams turned into nightmares and then into reality as Justin moaned in his sleep like he was being chased, and he thrashed around like he was struggling against invisible forces. His breath proved the plunging temperatures were below freezing and beyond cold. His skin was losing its warmth as frigid air was blown on him from something sinister and not visible to the naked eye. Something slowly scratched his back and shredded his t-shirt in the process, as drops of blood began to speckle through the back of his shirt. The top and bottom sheets were torn into thin ribbons of fabric with razor sharp claws belonging to a sinister being that intended to do much harm to Justin. Tangled in the shredded sheets, Justin tried frantically to get out of his bed since he was awake at this point and he was terrified at not knowing what was attacking him. Fear was consuming Justin.

Attempting to stand and remove the sheets simultaneously, he stumbled and fell on the floor, hitting his head hard in the process. He cut his forehead deeply when he hit his nightstand and then the floor. Blood was dripping down his face and pooling on the carpet beneath him. His breathing was steady, despite the trauma he just experienced. The shadow stood near the curtains and waited in the dark crevices of the bedroom as it watched Justin with the intensity of a snake about to strike. Justin wasn't moving, but his breathing hitched periodically, giving way to a possible emergency which no one could help with.

The shadow remained staring at Justin and would lock eyes if it could. It was surprised that Justin hadn't gotten up yet. It feared it put him through more than what he could handle. Justin was only human, after all.

The shadow needed to cause chaos elsewhere, so it quietly left, but not before giving Justin a nudge to see if he would move. Grunting, he slightly turned his head and stopped after he felt the puddle of blood that surrounded his head. His phone was somewhere close by, but he didn't have the strength to feel around for it. Not knowing how serious his injuries were was a cause for concern. Maybe he could call Andy to pick him up. He wasn't sure how he got on the floor, or why he had injuries in the first place. He looked for something out of the ordinary and didn't notice anything out of place apart from himself. Sun filtered through the windows in such a way that Justin knew he was late to work.

A knocking at the front door echoed throughout the house. Andy tried to call Justin, but he didn't answer. Not normally late to work without a phone call, Andy knew something must have happened, so he felt compelled to drive to his house. No noises could be heard from the inside and Andy was about to call the police when the front door opened on its own. Barely stepping inside, he looked around and didn't see Justin. He decided to call out to him.

"Justin! You home?"

Hearing muted sounds from upstairs, Andy ran up to them to see if Justin was okay. He peeked into his bedroom, turned on the light, and he caught his breath in his throat. Blood-soaked sheets were ripped to shreds, and Justin was barely visible around the edge of the bed.

"Justin!"

Andy rushed over to him to see what he could do to help. He saw all the blood and ran to the bathroom to get a couple of towels. He placed one over the bloody floor and one gently under Justin's head. He began to panic and felt queasy seeing all of all the blood.

"Justin, look at me. I need to see if you can focus on me. Do you know where all the blood is coming from? It's all over you and the bed, and I can't tell."

"I'm not sure. I see you though, I can focus my vision, but I feel really weak. Can you help me sit up?"

"Yeah, slowly." Andy put his arms underneath his and helped him sit up on the floor.

"My head hurts pretty bad. Can you see anything?"

Andy looked at Justin's head and the only injury he saw was the massive gash on his forehead.

"You've got a deep cut on your forehead. Other than that, it looks like your head is fine. You seem to have numerous scratches on your back and your shirt is shredded in several places. What got a hold of you?"

"I'm not sure. I honestly don't remember anything. Your guess is as good as mine," Justin said.

"Come on, let's get you to the hospital. You can't stay here like this," Andy said.

"Andy, I can't tell them the truth. It was likely the shadow that did this to me. I'm going to have to make up a stupid story about how someone invaded my home and attacked me in my sleep."

"Whatever you gotta do, Justin. We will worry about that later. We need to go."

Helping Justin up, then down the stairs proved to be tricky, but they managed. The front door remained wide open so they could easily exit. Andy helped Justin get in the front side passenger seat and he rushed to the driver's side to get in and get Justin to the hospital. The front door slammed shut after they drove away.

Eight

Checking in at the ER in the hospital proved to be easier than Andy thought. He grabbed Justin's driver's license and insurance card from his wallet for him and gave them to the receptionist at check-in. They immediately took him back, but didn't want Andy to go since he wasn't technically family. With Justin's insistence, and since he didn't have family here, Andy was the closest person to him. They finally conceded and let him go. They had a room to themselves that a doctor met them in. They proceeded to cut Justin's shirt off to remove it quickly, then they tended to his forehead. After they cleaned his wound, they determined that he did need about ten stitches. When the stitches were finished, they turned him over and tended to his back. Pouring antiseptic cleanser on his back made Justin wince, but he kept silent, only letting out a small groan of discomfort. Determining that he did not need stitches for his back, he relaxed a bit. They covered all the wounds with bandages and gave him a prescription for antibiotics.

The doctor asked several questions about what happened to him, and Justin was honest in the fact that he really didn't know what had happened. He assumed someone broke into his home, but he didn't notice anything gone. There wasn't anything else that he could add for the doctor. He assured him that he knew how crazy it sounded, but he was sound asleep in his bed when it happened, and he didn't actually remember being attacked. The doctor took notes and nodded as he spoke.

"Justin, I'm going to have to pass this along to the officer waiting out in the hallway. You'll need to talk to him. It's better to do this when everything is fresh in your mind and a couple of days later, even with the lack of details that you have about the attack itself at the moment. You might remember more after a couple of nights of good sleep." Dr. Sparks said that with genuine empathy. She seemed to feel bad for Justin, and the look of concern was real.

Dr. Sparks sent in the officer who took Justin's statement. Not feeling overly confident that they would catch the person or people that did this, he did offer one assurance.

"If they get caught from doing something else, it'll likely come out that they did this too. That's not much to go on, but it's something. Call me in a couple of days if you remember anything new. Thank you for your time, Mr. York."

The officer shook Justin's hand and walked out, taking a call at the same time. The doctor wanted him to stay overnight to be monitored since he hit his head. Fortunately, he was free to go home tomorrow morning, and he was looking forward to leaving the hospital. Going home however, he wasn't looking forward to encountering evil. Justin was grateful that Andy had grabbed a bag he kept at work for emergency trips, so he had a change of clothes and his toiletries. The lights were dimmed since he was going to attempt to take a nap. At this point in the day, it was late afternoon, and he was beat. He knew he needed the rest, but terrible things happened when he slept. He couldn't fight it any longer and he drifted off to sleep. Dreams came and went, but one nightmare lingered.

Fog filled the hospital room as the fluorescent lights flickered and buzzed. Dense fog seeped into the hallways after it filled Justin's room. Headstones popped up from the floor like they had been hidden there for decades. The roots from the pine tree grew out of the linoleum floor and twisted around the tombstones and ran the length of the room. In the far corner of Justin's hospital room, the church ruins materialized, and in the hallway red lights shone brightly like the house on the hill near the church.

The shadow stood near the walls of the church ruins watching Justin, contemplating its next move. It didn't have much time for what it needed Justin for. He was more resilient than it originally thought. Trying to wear him down has helped, but he was hoping to have broken his spirit by now. Moving closer to Justin, he kept his eyes on him. Running his claws down his body, he anticipated events in the next few days, but he had to be patient, which he wasn't used to.

Andy came in, and the shadow hissed and backed up. Sitting in the chair next to the bed, Andy patted his friend's hand and just wanted to be there for him when he woke up from his nap. The shadow was behind Andy and slowly reached both clawed hands out toward his neck and barely pricked him when Justin woke up, startled. The shadow and its world disappeared, as Justin became lucid.

"Ouch!" Andy rubbed his neck. He looked around, but didn't see anything. He saw a dot of blood on his fingers as he pulled them away from the back of his neck.

"Andy, you alright? Sorry, I drifted off; I'm not sure for how long. Have you been here awhile?"

"I'm fine, I guess I got bit by something. No, I just got here. Don't apologize, you need to rest."

"I can't stand that I have to stay the night. What time is it now? I don't see a clock and my phone is on that tray I can't reach."

Andy handed Justin his phone then sat back to continue talking to him. Looking at his phone, he saw that it was 7:00 p.m. The nurse that was assigned to Justin would be visiting soon to check his vitals, and he would get dinner shortly after. On the menu tonight was chicken alfredo, Caesar salad, a breadstick, and of course Jell-O and pudding. Justin ate his dinner, and Andy talked his ear off while he ate.

As they continued to talk after dinner, a storm was brewing outside. Only a couple of days away from Halloween, and it was fitting that a terrifying strong storm was looming over Stahl. Lightning strikes began and were getting closer together while the thunder grew increasingly louder. Both men looked toward the large window and noticed a raven sitting on the window ledge, black as the darkness surrounding it, and the black soulless depth of its eyes appeared to be staring directly at Justin. When the rain started to spit and hit the window, the raven flew away. Wolves began to howl from a distance, which was unusual, for Stahl only harbored coyotes and foxes. Andy and Justin looked at each other with concern. Andy rose from his seat to get a better view from the window. On the edge of the wooded area across the street, Andy saw three wolves pacing and a shadowed figure among the trees.

The Hounds of Hell crossed his mind as he walked back to his chair. He sat down and looked at Justin.

"There's three wolves and someone in the shadows across the street near the wooded area. I haven't a clue as to who that could be, but it's definitely creepy," Andy said.

"I have an idea who it is. That shadow that keeps bothering me while I'm awake and now in my dreams. It's likely him." Justin whispered like the shadow entity could hear him otherwise.

The fluorescent lights above them flickered off and on while the storm continued to rage outside. The hospital hallways and rooms were decorated for Halloween, which gave the place a uniquely sinister feel when the lights were momentarily out. Jack-o-lanterns adorned the patient rooms on the windowsills and the nurse's station both. Crepe paper hung in the hallway just outside Justin's room. Small and large plastic spiders were sprinkled everywhere imaginable.

Lightning struck nearby as the winds howled, and the trees thrashed against the windows while the lights abruptly went off. The only lights were from the jack-o-lanterns with small flickering tea light candles. The nurse at the station rushed to the phone to make calls about the lights. A loud crash was heard in the hallway, and when the hospital generators kicked in, the lights were up and running again, but the nurse had disappeared from Justin's doorway view. From where Andy was sitting, he could see feet being dragged and hidden behind the nurse's station.

"Um, Justin?"

"What's up, Andy?"

"Something weird is going on and I'm actually a bit scared, we need to leave," Andy whispered.

"Why?"

"Something happened to the nurse. I saw her feet disappear behind the desk area."

"Andy, I think you're right, we need to get out of here; help me up to get dressed."

Andy grabbed Justin's bag and brought it to the side of the bed that Justin was standing on. He pulled out sweats, boxers, t-shirt, a hoodie, and sneakers. While Justin got dressed, Andy put all his toiletries in the duffle bag and set his phone on top of it to ensure it would not get left behind. Grabbing his jacket and his own phone, Andy was ready to hurry out as quickly as possible. Justin had unhooked all the monitors that he had been hooked up to. He shoved his phone in his back pocket and put the duffle bag strap around him like a crossbody bag.

"I'm parked pretty close, so we should be able to get out rather quickly," Andy said as he motioned for Justin to follow him.

They were quietly leaving and shutting the patient room door without making a sound. Heading to the nearest elevators, they were able to get in without anyone else seeing them. The generators had enough juice to keep the elevators running, and Andy breathed a sigh of relief as they were able to get in one and go down to the lobby from the fourth floor. Unfortunately, the elevator ding was loud, and they had hoped that no one was around to see them exit the elevator. When the elevator door opened, they stood there for a few seconds to get their bearings. Looking around, they saw no one, again. Quickly and quietly they briskly walked to the entrance doors. Andy assured Justin his car was close. The storm was subsiding a bit outside and the rain had turned to drizzle. As the men neared Andy's car, they heard growls nearby. They looked toward the growls and noticed the three wolves across the parking lot staring them down. Behind them was the shadow. Nearly diving into Andy's car, they took off as fast as they could, heading to Justin's home.

Nine

When Andy pulled up to Justin's home, Justin jumped out to open the garage door, punching the code into the keypad. Andy got out of his car and grabbed all their stuff, locked the car, and followed Justin inside. Closing the garage door, they heard howling in the distance. The hounds of Hell were following them.

Justin immediately sat down on his couch to rest. Looking at Andy, he didn't miss a beat.

"Do you have anything new to tell me in regard to the research on the graveyard or church ruins?" Justin asked him.

"Actually, yeah. I found a common denominator with all the people buried at the Stahl Graveyard. Oh, and don't forget, we have Morgan's service tomorrow."

"Yes, go on please." Not wanting to waste any time, Justin encouraged him to talk fast.

"Well, I looked up all the individuals buried out there and the manner in which they died. They all had something in common," Andy said.

The howling of the wolves grew closer to Justin's home. Justin still wasn't feeling great, but his senses were heightened. He went around to make sure that all the windows were locked, curtains and blinds closed, all doors locked, and he shut all the lights off. Justin motioned for Andy to follow him to the office and to bring his phone. They quietly walked to the office and closed and locked the door. There weren't windows in Justin's office, so they couldn't tell where the wolves were. Justin knew they would try to get inside since they protected the shadow, even though he wasn't a threat.

"Andy, what were you going to say about the graveyard?"

"They all died in a violent manner. Every single person buried there. All of them were likely murdered at the hands of another. Since Morgan died in a terrible way also, it fits that she'll be buried there too. But what I still don't know is why this shadow thing is obsessed with you?"

"That's the question of the century. Or that this shit is even happening to begin with. Also, why Stahl?"

Justin was exasperated and tired of dealing with the craziness of this place. Doubt of choosing Stahl to settle down in was settling in every crevice of his being. He wanted to leave this place, but knew that it was not possible. The shadow would probably follow him anyway.

"You know, Justin. I think that the shadow and his hell-hounds are protectors of the lost souls at the Stahl Grave-yard," Andy said with confidence as he looked at Justin.

"Maybe. Or he's trying to keep their souls for himself," Justin said playing the devil's advocate.

They both sat in silence for a moment. Andy was scrolling on his phone, and Justin was lost in thought, staring off at his bookshelves.

"Andy, if I don't make it out alive from all this, you'll need to handle all of the arrangements for Morgan's service in the morning. I have a feeling that the shadow is not ever going to be done with me."

"Justin don't say that. You don't know what will happen. Maybe we can wait until this thing is out, and it will move on or just disappear."

"Ha! Not likely, but I appreciate your optimism."

The howling seemed incredibly close, and the scratching outside was magnified by the fact that there were three of them, which made it so much worse.

Whispers surrounded the house. Andy didn't seem to notice, but the deafening whispers to Justin were unbearable. He held his hands over his ears, scrunching up his face in pain and began to grunt and yell out as the whispers were never-ending and Andy was just a witness to something he couldn't understand.

"Justin! What's going on? What can I do?" He jumped up to stand next to Justin awkwardly.

"Make the whispers stop, *make them stop!*" Justin yelled.

"I don't hear anything Justin, I'm sorry. I'm not sure how to help," Andy said with empathy as he looked on at Justin helplessly.

Andy heard the wolves. They had made it inside the house and were outside of the office.

"Justin, do you hear that? The wolves are outside of the office door," Andy whispered.

Running his hands through his dark hair, which he did when he was anxious, Justin nodded to Andy in acknowledgement that he heard them. Not wanting to risk Andy's life, in an attempt to salvage him and his business, he decided that he would rush out of the office and close the door behind him, instructing Andy to remain there until he had heard nothing but silence for at least a few hours.

"Andy, I really want you to stay here. I'm going to leave the office and close the door. You lock it and stay put for a while. I have a phone charger in my desk you can use to charge your phone. You'll have to take care of Morgan's graveside service on your own. I'm sorry, but this is the only way I can keep you from getting even more involved, and even then there is no guarantee you'll be safe."

Andy nodded. He was ready to follow his orders. He hoped he could still meet Nicole for breakfast to catch up on everything, and she had offered to help him with the service.

"Ready?" Justin asked.

Andy nodded his head and was behind the door ready to lock it. Justin moved to the office door, unlocked it and stepped into the hall. He closed the door behind him and heard the growling immediately. He heard the lock click as Andy locked the door.

Good, thought Justin.

Walking to the living area, he stopped short when he was faced with the three wolves that were snarling, black as night, showing their razor-sharp teeth, dripping with blood on his carpet, protecting the shadow behind them.

Ah, Justin. You have come to your senses. I knew you would, eventually. You put up quite the fight though, I must admit. I need you now and you having to agree to submit to me is just glorious. We must go. Time is of the essence, and everything has to be done no later than midnight on Halloween.

Justin just looked at him, dumbfounded, not knowing what to say. He definitely did not want to leave with him, but he didn't really have a choice. Sighing, he nodded his head in agreement and moved to go outside. Walking slowly to the door, he looked back at the wolves, but they had disappeared as the shadow had. Scratching his head, he opened the front door and quickly closed it behind him. Stepping from the porch, he stood out in his yard, bewildered. He guessed maybe he was supposed to drive himself there, so he walked to the driveway where his car was parked to drive to the graveyard as he knew deep down that that is where he might remain.

Parking by the graveyard, he put his keys in the console and shut the door as he moved toward the headstones. He walked toward the pine tree as he assumed that was where the shadow would be waiting for him. He checked his phone, and it was nearly 3:00 a.m. Thursday morning. Sighing as he usually did, he continued, scanning the area for the shadow. He sniffed the autumn air and detected a faint odor of burnt human flesh. His stomach roiled and he tried to keep the vomit at bay. Taking deep breaths made it worse, so he tried to just breathe through his mouth as he waited and watched for the evil that awaited him. The dreaded anticipation was probably worse than what was likely in store for him.

Near the church ruins, the shadow lurked, waiting for Justin. Justin saw him and walked toward it cautiously. He still didn't feel well considering everything he had been through at the hands of the shadow in this world and in his nightmares. Fear overcame him as he realized the power that the shadow possessed. Shaking, he approached the shadow.

Don't fear me Justin. I have great things in store for you. We need to get started, but we must do it in the basement, so no one will see. I have so many fun surprises in store for Stahl!

Justin looked at the shadow, unable to find the words to convey what he was feeling. In all honesty, he probably already knew. The shadow moved slowly toward him until it was standing directly in front of Justin. It placed its gnarly, clawed hands around Justin's head and they disappeared together to the basement.

The basement was brighter this time than the last time Justin was there. There were lit torches in the corners, providing just enough light, but keeping the darkness near. A concrete throne was in one corner and a door partially open had evil hidden. A layer of dirt covered everything in the basement, including the floor. Crawling from out of the cracked door was a large tarantula, minding its own business, and skittering to find somewhere else dark to remain. Slimy burnt small hands reached out of the cracked doorway then completely emerged what was once a young woman, but now was an abomination at the hands of the shadow. Her mouth housed three rows of razor-sharp teeth and formed an enormous smile, a few strands of oily black hair that stuck to her pinkish burned skin that was covering her parasitic eyes, but resembled large iridescent yellow orbs. Her body remained human with burns covering her naked body with a fiery sinister glow, and she crawled toward Justin, inching closer and closer to him. She desired him, but in a sinister evil way that nightmares are drawn from.

The shadow was in charge of whatever was going on, and Justin was forced to be along for the ride. "Justin, there is another memory I need to show you. Well, a memory of mine."

The shadow put its clawed hands that appeared centuries old on Justin to show him its memory from Morgan's perspective so Justin could suffer even more. Human suffering is what brought the shadow immense euphoria.

Morgan was sitting under the monstrous pine tree, contemplating life, listening to music using her Air pods– she couldn't hear a sound. Approaching her from behind, the shadow stopped short of the pine tree and watched as curiosity seeped into the shadow, and he continued to observe her in silence. Gathering herself, she stood up to wander around the graveyard and explore the church ruins that Justin mentioned. Her deep-seated desire to find out things on her own was sometimes to her detriment. She knows she should've told Nicole and asked her to go, but she knew she would talk her out of it since Nicole was superstitious and looked for excuses to not be spontaneous, but she still was in love with her and hoped to spend the rest of her life in her arms at night. At the moment, she didn't have anything to lose but time. She walked around and looked at the ground near the remaining walls of the church and the cornfield next to it. She didn't see anything strange, but by the walls, an obscure spiral staircase leading to a basement was almost overlooked. Blending into the environment, growth had nearly made it invisible with weeds, dandelions, and vines that appeared to have roots leading to the basement. The crumbling gray walls had loose bricks, and some were scattered on the ground from decades of decay and neglect. She was fascinated by the area and understood Justin's obsession.

Using her cell phone as a flashlight, she bent down to have a look at the depth of the staircase. Shining what little light the phone put out illuminated the small area she was looking at, but proved to do very little as far as helping her be able to see anything of relevance. She bent over a little bit more, risking her ability to balance. The shadow crept up behind her and gave her a little nudge.

Losing her footing, she fell toward the depth of the basement floor. As she flailed to gain traction, she missed every time that she reached for the spindles of the archaic staircase, and she had no choice but to embrace the fear that exploded in her mind. Abruptly hitting the concrete floor, she lost consciousness and the use of her legs. The shadow was proud of its actions and knew that Morgan would be its prized pet to aid in its plan it had in store for Justin and Stahl both. It still needed to have a little fun. It conjured up a small ball of fire, throwing it up and down in its hands a few times, then dropped it on Morgan. She lit up like Epicurus in a flaming tomb. Startled, she screamed and thrashed around, but her legs were broken so she couldn't roll around to put out the flames. Her screams died on her lips once her nerve endings no longer had feeling, her organs no longer functioned, and she suffocated with the lack of oxygen. Her last gasp of breath was the shadow's first kill it had truly enjoyed in some time. When it knew someone mattered to others was when the kill was the sweetest to taste.

Hovering over Morgan, it ran its clawed hands over her burned body and inhaled the charred scent of the flesh that was still smoldering. Sticking its tongue out to get a little taste of Morgan's burned flesh from her face gave it shivers despite the heat from her body. Carrying Morgan's body, the shadow placed her under the pine tree so she could be found. It knew her funeral would be here, and it needed her final resting place to be where it took her life.

Taking its hands from Justin, the shadow waited for a reaction from him. Tears streamed down Justin's face when he saw that Morgan suffered much more than he had...so far.

"Why did you do that to her? She had her whole life ahead of her and she was a vibrant and kind person and people loved her!" Justin wanted to scream at him more, but he was tired, in pain, and had lost all hope for himself and Stahl.

"Precisely. I don't care who loves who or who is good and who isn't. That's not important to me, just you *humans* care about that."

Reaching down to acknowledge Morgan with a wave of its hand, the shadow also gave her a knowing glance to show it approved of her being so close to Justin. He flinched when Morgan touched his ankles and up toward his calves. She pulled at him, attempting to make him fall. He was able to shake her off and move away from her and the shadow both. The wolves were also nearby; Justin heard the howls and fear mixed with dread overcame him. The shadow cackled with amusement watching the fear in Justin's eyes, and knew he wouldn't be allowed to leave, probably ever.

Ten

Andy opened the mortuary early for Justin. He had no idea if or when Justin would show up, but he was meeting Nicole for breakfast and then they both would prepare for Morgan's graveside service afterward. They needed each other's friendship now more than ever. Nicole was having an especially difficult time. She felt guilty for the fight she had with Morgan. She wished she could apologize to her and have her back in her life.

Andy was waiting for Nicole in the lobby. He saw her pull up and a smile crossed his face. She was his closest friend in Stahl since Morgan was gone. He knew that Nicole felt the same. He watched her with fondness as she walked up and opened the door to enter the mortuary.

"Hey loser, how's it going this morning?" Nicole had a smirk on her face as she sat down next to Andy.

"Living the dream, like everyone else in Stahl," Andy blurted out, not planning to be so sarcastic.

Nicole forced a laugh and nodded in agreement. "Well, hey, asshole, give me a hug. I need it."

Andy stood up and embraced Nicole. They weren't in a hurry to end it; they both needed it. After several seconds, Andy broke the embrace and smiled at her and kissed her on the forehead. He gave her hands an affectionate squeeze and gently dropped them. They headed out the front door and locked up.

"Feel like the diner for breakfast? I don't know about you, but I could use a big country breakfast," Andy said while rubbing his belly with a goofy smile plastered on his face.

Nicole laughed, "Yeah. Sounds perfect as long as I can have unlimited amounts of black coffee."

"I don't see why that would be a problem." Giving her a wink, he opened his passenger side door for her.

Andy moved around to the driver's side and got in. He didn't notice the big black SUV that pulled out after him and followed him to the local diner. The drive was a short one, as the diner was only a street over. It was a trendy one, different than the one he and Justin usually went to. That one was old school, like a Waffle House. The one that he and Nicole were going to was small and independently owned. It was a boutique-style breakfast diner with modern aesthetics and Nicole loved it, so Andy wanted to take her there to give her a small amount of joy today.

Parking proved to be easy since it was so early. He pulled right up in front of the restaurant. The black SUV parked in the back of the parking lot, still undetected by Andy. Nicole nearly collided with Andy, eager to get coffee. They were seated right away, and Nicole didn't waste any time ordering coffee for them both as they looked at the menus.

"Everything looks so good. What do you think you're getting?" Nicole asked Andy.

"Um, the big country breakfast, literally." Andy smiled and Nicole nodded, remembering he had said that already back at the mortuary.

"I think I'm going to get the French toast with blackberries and cream. I've been dreaming about it because it's that good," Nicole said with anticipation.

The server walked up immediately after their conversation to get their order and top off their coffee. They ordered quickly and fell into a comfortable conversation about their memories of Morgan. Nicole regretted keeping their relationship a secret and should have been more open about being gay and loving another woman. Andy listened to every word and genuinely cared about Nicole's happiness. His heart broke for her, and he hoped that she could find love again when she was ready.

"It's easy in retrospect to wish you had made different decisions in your life. Trust me, I know this. All you can do is learn from them and try not to make the same mistakes again next time," Andy said, while placing his hand on top of hers and giving it a light squeeze.

The food they ordered arrived and they ate in silence because they were both famished. The server kept their coffee full and checked back on them often. It was the best service they had ever gotten there. The female server always glanced at Andy before walking away, lingering to catch another look at him. Nicole hadn't noticed, but Andy certainly did. He thought she was cute, and he decided to be bold and write his name and number on a clean beverage napkin. She seemed around his age, and she had beautiful hazel eyes, soft brown hair, and skin that he'd love to caress. He realized Nicole was asking him a question while he fantasized.

"Andy? Earth to Andy. Raven here wants to know if there is anything else we need?" Nicole asked, with an amused expression on her face.

"Oh, no I'm good, thanks. I'll take the check, please. He handed her the napkin, and after she read it, she looked back up to Andy, grinned, and nodded slightly.

"I'll be right back with your check, Andy." Raven smiled sweetly and walked away with a little bounce in her step.

"Oh, Andy, you sneaky little devil. Nice work, I'm impressed." They both laughed, enjoying this time together.

After Andy paid and briefly spoke with Raven to set up a date, they headed out to the parking lot. Nicole jumped in before Andy had an opportunity to be chivalrous and just waved him off. Smiling, Andy got in the driver's seat to head back to the mortuary, but not before he finally noticed the SUV. He was discreet, but he watched in the rearview mirror to see if he was indeed being followed and it was evident that he was.

Pulling into the mortuary parking lot by the door, Andy told Nicole to go ahead inside. He walked up to the SUV to the driver's side tinted window. The driver rolled it down and looked at Andy.

"Why are you following us?" Andy questioned, even though he was a bit nervous on the inside.

"We're looking for Justin York, your boss. Do you know where he is?" the mysterious driver inquired.

"Not exactly. He's either at his house or at the Stahl Graveyard. Why?" Andy asked the questions now.

"There's something he needs to be warned about, before it's too late."

"If you're referring to the wolves and the shadow man, it's probably already too late," Andy said with conviction and a touch of anger.

The man in the SUV just stared at Andy and opened his mouth to speak and closed it just as quick.

"Look, I understand how upset you must be. Yes, all of those things are a cause for concern, but there's more to it. You should be worried." He gave a final glance toward Andy and slowly drove away.

Andy waved him off and walked back to the mortuary to go inside and lock the door. He and Nicole wanted to make sure that everything was finalized for Morgan's service. Normally someone wouldn't simply be helping out for a service, but there was no one else who could assist him. If anyone asked, Nicole had taken a sudden interest in becoming an intern for the mortuary studying to be a funeral director. That was the best story they could come up with, knowing everyone knows everyone and no one would likely ask. She said she had an interest, so at least there was an iota of truth, even if it was a stretch. He asked Nicole to call the preacher to make sure that he would be on time and that he knew how to get there since he was quite old. Andy went to the columbarium room to retrieve Morgan's ashes. He found Morgan's urn rather quickly and carried her back to Justin's office, where Nicole was on the phone with the preacher. Setting the urn down on the coffee table in front of the love seat and two leather chairs, he walked across the room to Justin's desk. He needed to double-check the paperwork for the service, and he glanced at the computer screen and realized he needed to wake it up. The screen that popped up was a genealogy website. Justin had likely been working on figuring out his lineage, which Justin had kept from him.

Scrolling through the names of Justin's family, he noticed one that was familiar to him, and he sat back in the chair to remember where he had seen that name before. He knew it would come to him at some point soon. Justin had several articles about Stahl printed off with notes scribbled on them. He was impressed with the research that Justin had conducted. Just looking at everything, Andy wouldn't be surprised if Justin had figured out everything he was looking for already. Andy wondered if the guy in the SUV knew what Justin found out.

"Hey, Andy?" Nicole had a worried look on her face.

"What's up, Nicole?"

"We have a problem. The preacher can't get there before 5:00 p.m. He wrote down the three funeral services he had for today. The other two are at the newer cemetery right outside of town and he flipped-flopped the times for Morgan's and the 2:00 p.m. one there. He was so apologetic and really nice. I felt bad for him." Nicole's expression was one of concern and she was worried about Andy's response.

"Ahhhhh okay, so everything worked out. We don't need to stay here. Let's meet up here at 3:30. That gives us a couple of hours. Okay, I'll give Morgan's parents a call and see if they can wait until 5:00 p.m. Tomorrow is Halloween, and I really don't want to have the service then. This is wild and doesn't happen to Justin, like, *ever*."

"Andy, you sure there isn't anything else you need help with?" Nicole said.

"There's nothing else you need to do at the moment, so you can take a break. You know, I'll just give the Webber's a call in Justin's office, go on ahead. See you soon."

Andy went to the phone to give the Webber's a call. He had to look up their phone number, even though Justin likely had it memorized. He was like that. Justin took the time to get to know the families and called them several times, so it made sense that he would have the number memorized. Justin was a one-of-a-kind type of guy, and he truly hoped that he would come out of whatever evil had overcome him. Andy yelled out the front door at Nicole to come back into the office. She walked in, snacking on some fruit she had in her bag. Hanging up the phone after his call with the Webber's, he looked at Nicole.

"What'd they say?" Nicole asked.

"The call went well. They weren't planning on having anyone over to the house for a wake and didn't schedule a lunch afterwards. So fortunately, it will be fine as far as timing. We should be there by 4:00 p.m. with the urn."

Nicole nodded her head in agreement and headed out. Andy was right behind her, and he locked up the mortuary. He looked around to see if the black SUV was around, but he didn't see it. Guessing that the rude, mysterious SUV driver only had business with Justin, he figured he was safe. He looked forward to the break between now and Morgan's service. Andy tried to call Justin and just got his voicemail again. Hopefully he will hear back from him soon.

At the Stahl Graveyard, Nicole met Andy at 4:00 p.m. like he had said to do. Andy had gotten here even earlier. It would be a quick service and there was no need for a tent and chairs since there would only be a few of them, plus it was a nice evening. There was a slight breeze, and the sun was still shining. It was an unseasonably warm October day. The day before Halloween proved to be a busy one in town, so Andy opted to leave early for the graveyard. The small town was out shopping for last minute costumes, candy, and décor, which meant traffic would be brutal. While he waited for everyone else to get there, he and Nicole decided to go explore, since they had time. They talked more about their good memories of Morgan while they looked around the church ruins. As they were checking everything out, they noticed something on the ground that looked out of place. Nicole bent down by the crumbling wall and picked up a cell phone. She held it up for Andy, who took it and looked it over.

"That's Justin's phone. He must have dropped it here by accident. I have no idea where he is."

"Obviously he was here, but where is he now?" Nicole asked, looking around for him and any other clues.

Andy saw something strange on the ground that he nearly overlooked.

"Hey, look at this!"

He brushed dirt and leaves away that surrounded a winding staircase leading to a basement that probably once had belonged to the church.

"Nicole, you think that Justin fell down there? I bet he did, which would explain why we haven't heard from him."

"Justin! Hey, are you down there? Can you hear me? Make some noise if you can!" Andy yelled out, in hopes of hearing something. He bent over as far as he could without falling into that inky abyss.

Andy and Nicole waited for a reply. All they heard was deafening silence and then corn stalks brushing up next to each other in the wind breaking the momentary silence. Andy got up and stuck Justin's phone in his pocket; he would drop it off at the mortuary later after the service. Worry washed over him as his mentor seemed to be missing. He and Nicole decided to walk back to Morgan's grave. Walking back downhill, they both saw the house on the hill that Justin mentioned. Red glowing lights appeared from every window. They saw a shadowy figure near the grove of trees that lined the back of the house. It didn't appear to be the owner and fear settled in. Assuming it was something sinister in nature and not wanting to alert it of their presence, they quietly continued to the grave to wait for Morgan's parents and the preacher.

Mr. and Mrs. Webber greeted Nicole and Andy respectfully. They waited in silence for the preacher to show up. They periodically looked over where everyone parked, assuming he would drive up any second as it was rapidly approaching five o'clock.

Mrs. Webber was beginning to worry. "Do you think he forgot? He's going to be late, and we're just standing here not doing anything. The grave diggers are waiting as well."

"Mrs. Webber, I understand your concern, and I am so very sorry. There's nothing we can do but wait patiently for a bit longer. Let's give him just a little more time." He gently squeezed her shoulder and gave her an apologetic look.

Nicole noticed something on the hill out of the corner of her eye. She thumped Andy on the shoulder to get his attention.

"Look. Who's leaving the creepy house?" Nicole asked.

Dripping with sarcasm, Andy was losing his patience as he spoke. "Probably the guy that lives there."

Shooting Andy a warning look Nicole replied, "Thanks, Captain Obvious."

The man who had left the house was walking directly toward them at a steady pace. The closer he got, the more uncomfortable everyone else became. He was an elderly white man, with beads of sweat on his upper lip and sweat dripping down the side of his face. He was dressed in a nice suit, which explained why he was sweating. He extended his hand to the Webber's.

"Mr. and Mrs. Webber, it's lovely to finally meet you. I'm preacher Barnes."

"Oh, nice to meet you too. We had no idea that you lived in the house on the hill," Mrs. Webber spoke up, changing her tone for the man of God.

"Yes, I don't disclose that to anyone. Some people get curious and come knocking on my front door, but if I'm home, I usually ignore it. I just don't feel like being overly social these days," preacher Barnes said as he caught his breath.

"Well, shall we get started?" Preacher Barnes asked.

Everyone nodded in agreement, so he began the service. Brief didn't even begin to cover it. He read the eulogy that Mrs. Webber wrote, he shared a few family stories and ended with a sermon that was generic in nature. Morgan's parents

remained solemn, while Nicole tried to hold back her sob-
bing, but failed miserably because her heart was shattered in
a million pieces. Andy let a few tears escape that rolled down
his cheeks. He was raised to believe that real men don't cry.
He was very different than what his family expected, but he
learned a long time ago to stop giving a fuck about others'
expectations of him.

Everyone thanked preacher Barnes after the service. Andy
told Morgan's parents that he would stay and oversee the
grave as the grave diggers put the dirt back to cover up the
outer burial container with the urn. They felt that was a great
idea and quickly left.

"Andy, do you need me to stay with you?" Nicole asked.

"No, you can head out. Thank you for all your help today,
I really appreciate it. I know the entire day was difficult for
you, even though you couldn't show all the emotions you
felt." Andy hugged Nicole tightly and gave her his usual hand
squeezes. They looked at each other and knew their friendship could withstand anything, considering what they just
went through.

"Thank you Andy, for being there for me and including me
in everything today. Your friendship has become so important to me, you're like family now." Nicole smiled at him and
walked backward for a moment and blew him a kiss. Sighing,
she gazed at Morgan's grave and quietly muttered, *you have
broken me and there is nothing left in my heart.* Wiping tears

away with her hands, she turned and finished her walk to her car.

Andy watched her leave, making sure she was okay when she drove off. He turned just as the preacher was walking back up the hill to go home. He wished Justin was here because he missed him and was worried about him. He hoped and prayed he got to see Justin again, they had a lot of catching up to do. He needed his friend and mentor back; he didn't like holding down the fort so to speak. Tears pricked his eyes while he thought about Justin. He felt pretty good about handling the service himself, but the looming fear was still hanging over him like a dark cloud. At least now he knew he was capable of handling things. He thought he would grab his favorite pizza and crack open a beer when he got home. By the time he was able to leave the graveyard, it was after 7:00 p.m.

The next evening while darkness swallowed the sun, dirty little secrets were falling from lips at parties, where the alcohol flowed and clothes were coming off. Very few worried about sinful behaviors. Some of the adults in Stahl had more fun on Halloween than the children. Halloween was now in full swing with all the festivities. Skeletons adorned many yards and porches were lit with jack-o-lanterns. Spiders hid in bushes and trees with the webs they wove for their victims innocently awaiting their next meal. Screams and haunted house noises blasted from homes while the trick-or-treaters ran from house to house, getting as much candy as possible. Parents not at the adult costume party in town pulled their Radio Flyer wagons, following their kids while hoarding their flasks and snacks to cope with the stress of the holiday expectations that came with being a parent.

The house on the hill was lit up with the sinister flickering of red lights casting shadows on the gray home, with peeling paint and aged window sills. Grass had grown up around the home and alluded to the idea of neglect. Preacher Barnes was nowhere to be seen, but he knew what awaited Stahl. He bargained with the devil for his quiet life of solitude. The shadow wreaking havoc emerged feeling victorious even before its plans were put in motion. The shadow sided with the side of silence as he quietly watched and waited for his time to strike. Stahl wasn't ready, nor would it ever be. Justin stood beside it, not by choice, but by force. What used to be Morgan lay at the shadow's feet, obeying every directive thrown her way.

As midnight approached, the shadow was giddy with the excitement building up in its wicked and dark soul. What it would unleash could not be undone. What Justin would become would take a miracle to shatter. The evil that would envelop Stahl was near and would conquer all that remained innocent and pure. Vitriol and hate for humanity would become apparent after midnight. Justin was key, because of his lineage. The shadow needed him to grow stronger and to watch all other humans become weak with fear and hopelessness. It's what fed it and kept it at peace with the pace of events. Justin was a descendant of Margaret Whittier, who was accused of witchcraft. Making Justin a warlock would give the shadow the strength needed to rule the world.

The shadow headed down to the graveyard and Justin followed. Morgan slowly crawled her way down to the graveyard behind them. The wolves remained nearby. Once the shadow was among the headstones in front of the pine tree, it began to chant.

My children, rise and become one
Your eternal rest is no more
We will rule together and become—
Leaders of the world
I am your God, your Devil,
Everything you need me to be
Rise and join me to overcome
Stahl, and they will serve me
Rise my children, rise!

The shadow repeated the chant multiple times. At midnight, the souls of the damned in the Stahl Graveyard rose from their graves. Every soul that was tortured, set ablaze, raped, and murdered, would now get their revenge in the afterlife. The shadow grabbed Justin by the shoulders, and it entered Justin's body as it had practiced over the last several days, to ensure that Justin's body could withstand the drastic change he was about to endure. Justin's soul was now lost to the devil as they became entwined as good and evil within one body. Justin transformed into an unsightly being with horns protruding from his forehead, his hands became elongated with black claws like monsters from nightmares, and his skin was a gray pallor like he had never seen the sun. His beautiful blue eyes were now black as onyx. Justin, in essence, became the devil. There were faint features that would remind others of Justin, but he was born anew. The shadow turned innocence into evil with ease. The souls that had been wronged, murdered by the hands of another, now belonged to the devil and their thirst for revenge was paramount. They were making their way to Stahl together, an unbeatable force of nature and abominations. Preacher Barnes watched safely from his house on the hill, staying safely hidden earlier from all prying eyes. He knew there was nothing he could do that would stop the evil that would infest Stahl and beyond.

The ghosts from the graveyard and Justin began their walk to town to destroy anyone and everything in their path, unless they agreed to join them. Eighty ghosts and Justin made their way through the streets of Stahl and killed everyone in their path, which wasn't many, due to the witching hour being upon them. They could freely enter homes and invade the sleeping innocent and the guilty alike.

There must have been a little bit of Justin left, because as a few of his ghosts were about to enter Andy's home, he screamed at them that that particular home was off limits, and they needed caretakers of the dead. He and Nicole were not to be touched. Stopping in their tracks, they backed away from Andy's home. Justin struggled to remain present in his body because he could feel the malignant evil spread its fingers throughout his insides. He knew his hours or days were numbered and he would slowly fade permanently in the background as the devil took over every crevice of his body and brain. It took what little strength he had to protect Andy and Nicole. Moving through the street that Morgan's parents lived on, several ghosts entered their home and Justin followed. They were asleep in their bed since it was nearly 3:00 a.m. The ghosts made sure that they couldn't leave the bedroom so the devil could do as he wished.

"Wake up, Mr. and Mrs. Webber. I have a surprise for you." Shaking them awake, Mrs. Webber screamed, and Mr. Webber looked confused while he tried to understand what was going on around him.

Crying, Mrs. Webber could not be consoled. Overwhelmed with fear as she looked around their bedroom, she saw with clarity that they were going to die, but she couldn't understand why this was happening.

"Why? Why is this happening? I don't understand!" Mrs. Webber continued to cry.

"Well, Mrs. Webber, why *not*? But, if you *really* need an explanation. Here's one for you. I am darkness, I am evil, I want to rule. So, you're either with me, or against me. What do you think?" He waited for a response from her.

"I can't join you in your evil escapades. You are the embodiment of everything I detest!" Her voice quivered with fear.

"Suit yourself," The devil said, as he moved closer to her and stared her in the eyes and gripping her soul.

She thought she saw a glimmer of something familiar, but decided that wasn't possible.

Mr. Webber looked over at his wife; they whispered "*I love you*" to each other. They held each other's hands tightly, gazing into each other's eyes. They prayed quietly, knowing the end was coming.

The devil closed in on Mrs. Webber first. Standing in front of her, looking her up and down and then staring directly into her eyes, he reached into her chest cavity and pulled out her beating heart. Grinning with satisfaction, he was amazed at his own strength, and excitement took over as he bit into her heart, slightly clenching it in his hands as he chewed. Blood dripped from both his mouth and his fisted hand. Mrs. Webber collapsed back on the bed as Mr. Webber screamed endlessly until the devil backhanded him to shut him up. Mr. Webber fell back, knocked out cold with gashes across his face. The wounds were deep, and blood now soaked the sheets he lay upon. Mr. Webber was still breathing, but shallow breaths were all he could manage. Justin stood over Mr. Webber and studied him intently. Deciding he was done with him, he slowly slit his throat from one side to the other. Blood spilled even more and flowed freely. Any internal glimmer of Justin that remained was no longer there, as he licked and tasted the coppery blood with his tongue, closing his eyes as he enjoyed becoming a monster. It missed this. As a shadow, it was limited to what it could do. Now its power had the life force that no mere man could destroy.

Leaving the Webber's home, Justin and his ghosts were moving on to the next home, but not before Justin lit a Zippo lighter he found next to an unlit cigar in their living room and set their curtains ablaze. Everyone here was no longer living, yet he loved fire even though no one would die from it. He put the Zippo in his pocket and left through the front door, not bothering to close it. A few teenage boys were walking down the street with cans of beers in their hands and cigarettes in their mouths. They stopped and watched the fire consume the house, not noticing all the ghosts in the street and the devil next to them. Sirens could be heard in the distance, and the boys didn't want to stick around and be accused of this. Starting down the street, they turned to walk and ran into the devil.

"Hey man, watch where you're going!" One of the teenagers yelled at the devil.

"Oh, am *I* in *your* way?" the devil asked the mouthy teen.

"Fuck yeah, you *are* freak! Like, Halloween is basically over. Take your costume off, you weirdo!"

The boys waited for the devil they thought was wearing a costume to do something.

"Well, the thing is, I can't take this off as it's me, not a costume." Gesturing toward his entire body.

The boys laughed until the devil grabbed one of them by the throat, lifted him up off the ground, and threw him across the street.

"Who's next?" he asked the boys.

The boys ran off and tried to grab their friend across the street, but he wasn't moving. He hit his head on bricks that surrounded a flowerbed. One of the boys kept pushing him to get up, and noticed the blood pooling at the back of his head. Both boys gasped when they realized their friend was gone. The remaining two boys ran away as fast as they could and disappeared behind a house a block away. The devil needed to figure out its next move, so it conjured up a small ball of fire and chucked it at the boy. It landed on the dead boy.

Perfect, it thought as the flames grew and consumed the boy.

The devil climbed a large elm as high as it could go next to the house that was now an inferno. It was still dark, but the morning sun would be arriving in a couple of hours. It needed to hide so the firemen didn't see it. It hadn't decided if it would kill them or not—tonight.

Exacting revenge on a town using the ghosts that craved revenge for their own demise, was a ruse for its plan which no one else knew. All the ghosts that needed to take revenge had their justice, making what was a small town much smaller. The ghosts would have to return to the graveyard before dawn. Once a year it could resurrect the spirits, and they could walk the streets of Stahl together. There was one spirit that it had hoped it could force to stay here forever.

While watching the firemen that had just arrived, it was contemplating its next move. The firemen worked quickly to put out the fire that it had purposely started. One of the firemen noticed the teen boy that lay unmoving across the street. They called 9-1-1 for an ambulance while they tried unsuccessfully to revive him. After the paramedics and the police officers arrived, they determined that he tripped and hit his head after he set the fire. They didn't feel it necessary to open an investigation because it appeared to be an open and shut case.

Stupid humans, the devil thought.

At this point, the few neighbors that were still alive had stepped outside in their pajamas to see what all the commotion was. They watched and whispered about the fire and the boy. The homes were far enough apart that no other homes were damaged in the fire. The devil observed the few neighbors while the details of its plan consumed his thoughts. It needed to return to the graveyard, but it waited until the neighbors returned to the comfort of their homes first. It slowly climbed down the tree and jogged undetected back to its home in the graveyard.

The ghosts were roaming the graveyard when the devil returned. It approached one, as time was running out before the sun would rise and they would all rest again. Standing before the ghost of Margaret Whittier, it asked for her help since she likely knew the answer to its question.

"If I could bring you back to life, would you rule with me?" the devil asked.

In a soft and wispy voice, "If I can have freedom to do what I'd like, whenever I'd like, then the answer is yes." Margaret's ghost stood facing the devil and waited for whatever came next.

"We need the souls of children to make that happen. We will sneak into the homes, and you can suck the life out of them and that will give you *your* life back. I have a spell that you will have to chant with me so you can make this happen since it's almost sunrise." The devil looked at her with hope that she would agree.

The ghost of Margaret Whittier nodded her head in response and agreed to do it. The devil began to recite his spell for Margaret's transition.

Soul for a soul is what is needed for life
Taking one and breathing for a price
Sinister deeds will run amok
Death and destruction is a must
Conniving and deceit is needed, not luck
Evil in darkness will corrupt—
the end is near for the human race
Ending lives ends in grace—
for Margaret

Margaret looked at the devil and said, "Let's be clear, we are family with the same blood line, I will not serve you. We will have an equal partnership."

"Of course, this is the only way. We must leave now."

They were able to travel quickly. The first home they chose had three children. They chose the twelve-year-old girl since the older children were stronger and slept later than the younger ones. Margaret straddled her in her bed, leaning over her, and began to suck the life out of the young girl through her mouth. The girl was suffocating as Margaret took her soul. Tears streamed down her face, and she had a look of sheer terror in her eyes as she attempted to take her last breath. The look of terror remained, and her corpse was pale and slightly shriveled. Satisfied with what they'd accomplished, they moved on to the next child in another home.

On the same street, but five houses down on Devil's Road, aptly named, they approached their next home to quietly invade. They chose the oldest child again, but this boy was fourteen and much larger than the last victim. They were both giddy with excitement. Margaret straddled the boy and began to suck his soul through his mouth and inhaled deeply. He awoke, shuddered in shock, and began to buck underneath Margaret. The devil had to step in and swat him across the face, leaving claw marks that stunned him still. Margaret finished and the boy's eyes rolled up toward the back of his head, his body relaxed, and he was still and stiff forever.

The last home on the same street they chose had one child. He was ten and sleeping in. They approached him the same as the others. However, he was on the verge of waking up as it was nearly 6:00 a.m. and that was the norm for him. Margaret crept up toward him and he suddenly popped his eyes open. He screamed and jumped out of bed. He yelled out for his parents.

The fearful boy screamed, "Mom! Dad! Help me! I'm scared!"

"Yell all you want boy, your parents won't hear you," the devil hissed.

It grabbed him and took him to the kitchen where his parents were. They were sitting at the table having coffee which had turned cold. Both his parents had claw marks across their faces and their throats had been slit from one side to the other. Blood covered their clothes and the table alike. The boy screamed again. The devil put its clawed hand over his mouth to stifle the screams. Margaret stood in front of him and as soon as the devil removed its hand, she sucked his soul right from his body. It didn't take long since he was small for his age and quickly gave up on fighting.

Quickly and quietly, they left through the back door and walked back to the graveyard. They walked all the way to preacher Barnes' home and just let themselves in without knocking.

The devil called out in annoyance since the preacher wasn't visible when they went inside.

"Preacher! I need you! Come here, now," the devil yelled.

They waited, but he didn't show. The devil decided to look for him, and he didn't have to go far. He slammed open his bedroom door just as preacher Barnes was zipping up his pants. He threw money on his bed at the young woman who lay naked on top of the comforter and fluffy pillows. The devil looked surprised, but pleased.

"Well, you don't see that every day. Nice work preacher Barnes! Come downstairs, I have someone for you to meet."

"Ok. Where are all the ghosts and your pet, Morgan?"

"They all are back in their final resting place until next Halloween."

They both went downstairs, and Margaret was waiting in the entryway close to the front door.

"Preacher Barnes, this is Margaret Whittier."

They shook hands and then preacher Barnes looked startled because he recognized the name.

"How?" Preacher Barnes asked.

"You don't want to know. But good news. We are moving in."

Stahl was an extremely small unincorporated community. Lawrence was close by and had thousands of college students available to them if they chose to use The University of Kansas as their next playground. Blissfully happy, the devil said to Margaret, "We live, and we die in the shadows, but darkness always wins."

The End

Acknowledgements

Thank you to my family for putting up with my crazy schedule between teaching and writing, I know it's a lot. A special thanks to my editor at Marked Up Editing, Meriah Gutterson. You're kind and generous and so easy to work with. Thank you Stephanie Huddle for the Beta read and developmental edits. Your generosity knows no bounds and I treasure our growing friendship. Thank you Christy Aldridge at Grim Poppy Design for my wonderful cover. You are always a joy to work with, and your kindness doesn't go unnoticed. For Savannah R. Fischer, thank you from the bottom of my heart for doing the interior art and the formatting and for being an amazing friend. Your work is beautiful! Thank you to the Scribes group, especially Jyl Glenn for your friendship, chaos wrangling, and inclusive heart, all while answering my questions. Scribes, you know who you are, and I love you all. I would be remiss if I didn't thank Matt Rayner for answering endless questions and your friendship. Thank you Andrea and Sara for keeping me laughing, I appreciate you both. Thank you to the ladies in the best Patreon, you keep life fun, and I love you all. To my readers, I appreciate you reading my work; that is what keeps me going and what makes this worthwhile. Thank you JosnDee Photography for my author photos, I love them and working with you both is beyond fun. And finally, a special thank you to Andrew Scott for meeting with me and sharing your experiences as a mortician and a Funeral Concierge. The education required and the industry in general is truly fascinating.

Author's Note

This story was inspired by the urban legend surrounding the Stull, Kansas graveyard and former church, and pine tree that used to adorn the small town. Stull isn't a town any longer, it's unincorporated and very few residents remain. Numerous accounts of strange occurrences have been documented and whether they are true or not, remains to be seen. A few of those accounts are sprinkled in the novella. It has been said the location was one of seven gateways to Hell with the devil showing up Halloween and Summer Solstice to take people back to Hell with him. The graveyard is now private property and gated off with numerous no trespassing signs due to vandalism. The University of Kansas is about fifteen to twenty minutes away and college students would party there. I do plan to visit before the release of this novella.

Resources:

Hefner Heitz, Lisa. *Haunted Kansas*. 1997. University Press of Kansas

www.americanhauntingsink.com

www.theculturecrush.com

About the Author

Kristal Shanahan writes spooky stories late at night with coffee in hand and music in her ears. When she isn't encouraging her dogs and cat to play nice, she's spending time with her sweet family and friends. Her stories can be described as atmospheric with a touch of gore, in the vein of traditional horror tropes.

Connect with Kristal here:
Facebook: Kristal Shanahan-Author
Instagram: @Ladyinhorror_author
TikTok: @Ladyinhorrorwriting
Website: www.ladyinhorror.com